Chro

Written by
Mason Good-Turney

Edited with the assistance of
ChatGPT
AI Language Model by OpenAI
and Matt Brown

Cover Illustration by
Savanna Harmon
@siren_of_art.20

Published with KDP Publishing

Copyright 2024 Mason Good-Turney

Dedicated to
Val and Ellie, I love you both
more everyday.

Table of Contents

1. Creation and Brief History of Edoria
2. Northland
3. Oranna of the North
4. River Gale
5. The Rescue of Princess Bajaw
6. Voyage to the Isle of Forgotten
7. The Fool King
8. The Trials of Horvath
9. Colossal Beast
10. Fight on Black Sands

Creation and Brief History of Edoria

In the beginning, the world was dark and void. Then, a flash of brilliant light streaked across the sky, setting into motion a metamorphosis. The world began to shake and tremble, with each seismic shift masses of land rose and crashed out of the sea. As the light faded, the brightest of these hung in the air and illuminated the new land. This new light brought warmth to the land and dried it. The masses, still shifting in their infancy, crashed into each other, creating mountains and inland lakes. Some mountains cracked open, and hot lava spewed from these openings with creative violence and destruction. Each eruption caused huge ash clouds to cover the world, and the world warmed.

Time passed, and the land masses settled, forming several large continents on this virgin world. Mountains, jagged and snow capped, reached to the far north and stretched down the coasts. Rivers flowed to the coasts, carving up the land, bringing a lifeline that created lush fields, deep forests and rolling meadows.

One day, the sky became dark, and fire rained from the heavens. In the atmosphere, a large comet flew in front of the brilliant light, bathing the world in darkness. As the comet passed, bits of the comet broke free and crashed into the land, creating craters all over the world. The tranquil land burned and shuddered with each impact.

When the dust settled and the comet had passed, all was quiet as light filled the air once again. But not all was calm. Deep within the craters, something stirred. The fragments of the celestial comet fused with the living soil of the world, and from this fusion emerged the race of Giants.

The Giants that emerged gained power related to their birth craters. The Earth Giants lived in the fields and forests. Using their power, they grew crops and cultivated the land, making it rich and vibrant.

The Water Giants lived on the coasts and on the islands in the sea. Their power was used to wash and purify the land.

The mountain giants lived throughout the world, using rocks to make gemstones and metals. But they were also able to use magma from the earth to create or destroy new land.

The last species of Giants were the Sky Giants. They lived high in the mountains, so high they were able to touch the clouds. They built vast kingdoms upon the clouds. It is even said they were able to travel the stars. The sky giants used their power to create lightning, thunder, and rain. All four giant species lived in isolated harmony, with each race being drawn to each other but staying in their respective realms.

For an age, the Giants lived in peace, until one day the water giants discovered a new skill. They found that by willingly sacrificing a part of their life force, they could create life. Using this gift, they created the race of Elves, finding love and joy from their creation. The Water Giants placed them on islands and helped cultivate their civilization. They nurtured the Elves and taught them to fish and sail.

Soon, the Elves' numbers grew larger than the island could hold. The Water Giants constructed arcs and showed them the way to the mainland. As their first ships landed, the Elves gave thanks to their creators and named the land Ed-Oria, meaning New Blessing.

The Elves began to construct small settlements on the coast and ventured down rivers. A group known as Ilithinians explored past the coasts and into the forests. There, they found the home of the Earth Giants.

The Earth Giants were surprised and confused to see these creatures. They were even more surprised to hear them speak in their tongue. Upon learning that their brothers had created intelligent life, the Earth Giants attempted this feat. With the knowledge learned, they brought forth the great beast races and scattered them throughout the world. To a select few they gave, reasoning and intelligence transforming them into the Wildfolk, beasts that walk on two legs.

The Wildfolk and Elves formed great bonds, living amongst each other as equals. To celebrate their society, each year the Earth and Water Giants had the great Feast of Life. At the feast, the Giants decided they would bring their creations to their brothers, the Mountain Giants. The Elves and Beastfolk gathered gifts and treasures they had created to bring to the Mountain giants. On the 3rd moon, a great caravan of Elves and beastfolk journey into the mountains.

When they found the Mountain Giants, they were met with fear, disdain, and jealousy. For the first time since the time of Nothing and the Emergence, the harmony and peace was disrupted. The Mountain Giants cursed their brothers and drove them out of their domain. Out of hate, the Mountain Giants tried to form their own life. Without the full understanding, they created the race of Monsters.

Monsters poured into the forests and coasts of Ed-Oria, burning and killing as they came. Feeling the pain of their creations, the Earth and Water Giants marshaled their powers to go to war. Seeing the destruction forced into the world, one of the Mountain giants forsook, his brothers and offered himself as a sacrifice to the Earth and Water Giants. Through this sacrifice, a race of formidable beings emerged to aid the Elves and Beastfolk, the Dwarves were born. With the aid of the

Dwarves, the Elves and Beastfolk were able to push back the monsters. Driven back to the shadows, the Monsters and Mountain Giants hid, and for a short time peace through war was obtained.

    Before too long, the Mountain Giants grew hungry for war and once again marshaled their forces to attack. This time, they, through dark magic, unleashed their fiercest monsters, the Dragons. The armies of the Mountain Giants marched on the world. The Water Giants and Earth Giants pushed back with their forces, and the conflict was a standstill. With blood shed on both sides, no end to conflict was insight.

    The Giants called a Great Council to figure out a way to end the conflict. As they gathered, their talks soon turned to arguing and fighting, and nothing could be decided upon. They withdrew from the council and prepared for a great battle. As the two sides rushed to meet, a bolt of lightning struck the battlefield. Its force shook the ground and knocked the combatants down. The dust settled, and before them stood the Sky giants. Everyone stared in awe. No one living had ever seen the Sky giants. They had heard whispers from the other giants, but nothing prepared them for this.

All the while, the world bound giants fought their brothers, the Sky Giants studied the stars and heavens. They helped their brothers up and presented them with a treaty. The Sky Giants used their power to create Man. Into Man, they offered all of the Giant's abilities and knowledge. With man now living on earth, the race of Giants would ascend to live in the sky and let their creations rule themselves. Upon hearing this they agreed.

Each giant race added to the creation of man. The Water Giants offered exploration and the need to discover the unknown. The Earth Giants offered a love for land and creatures of the world. The Mountain Giants, to spite the others, offered the knowledge of mortality and an unquenchable lust for power. The Sky Giants offered wisdom and reason. There on the battlefield, all the Giants ascended into the heavens. This new creature breathed its first breath and rose to its feet, and so began the Age of Man.

NORTHLAND

In the north where the sleeping giants lie
The warriors way has all but passed by
Your sword sings your song
Your life to prolong

Where eagles soar way up high
While the sun shines in the sky
When your luck runs out
Your life you are without

Whether in the mountains so cold
Searching for treasures of gold
The swords code is how you die
In the north where the sleeping giants lie

Found on a tablet in the Great
Mountains
Unknown Author

Oranna of the North

Oranna woke to the smell of smoke and the sound of clashing metal. Quickly, she grabbed her urgrosh. Gulping a drink from her drinking horn, the liquid rolled down her throat giving her a boost of energy. Taking a breath, she threw back the furs that served as her door and stepped into chaos. Her village was being attacked by a raiding party from the south. Raiders usually attacked weaker villages to acquire slaves or men for the mines, but she had never heard of them coming this far north.

An armored soldier rushed at her with a drawn sword, but she easily blocked his attack and cleaved into his neck. As he fell, the two soldiers following him turned and fled from her fierce strength. After all, she was Oranna of the Northern Mountain tribe.

While she searched for those who needed her help, Oranna heard the beat of hoofs, but she couldn't see through the thick smoke. Quickly, she ducked behind a building to avoid being spotted, but it was too late. Three large cloaked creatures on horseback appeared from the smoke and cornered her.

Never fearing a challenge, she launched her attack. However, to her surprise, these creatures moved quickly. Each missed swing drained her spirit. As she faced two of them the third creature crept up behind Oranna, grabbed one of her arms. Oranna swiftly threw it and with a swing took its hand. Her triumph turned to defeat as the other two lassoed her with ropes and tied her down. Trapped, she didn't have enough strength to break free.

The creatures regrouped, tending to their injured comrade, and then dragged Oranna forcefully to the awaiting wagons. As they tossed her in, she noticed that they had only managed to capture a third of the village. A glimmer of hope sparked within her mind, as she hoped that the others had escaped.

However as the wagons left and the smoke cleared, the carnage became evident, and her hope faded. Oranna sat in her cage, filled with despair as anger and pain coursed through her veins.

The caravan of slaves traveled for hours, and Oranna noticed that there was only one other person in her cage. He didn't look familiar, and when he smiled at her, she let out an audible scoff.

He appeared to be a human, standing around 5'11" with short, brown hair that was dirtied from sleeping in the hay. His eyes were hazel with gold circles around the pupils, and he sported a short brown beard with hints of red and a touch of gray. Above his right eye, he bore a scar, probably from a childhood fall. His broad shoulders made him look strong like a fighter but his smile was gentle like a scholar. Oranna paid him little attention. As the caravan rumbled on, she wondered what fate awaited her.

"How'd they catch you?" he asked. "I'm looking around at the guards, and it seems like they're missing some. And these others in the cages don't look like warriors. So, how did they catch you?"

Oranna sighed, not eager to speak, but feared if she didn't answer her cellmate would continue to pester. "Two cloaked creatures took me by surprise," she answered.

"I thought they had three creatures," he replied, sounding puzzled.

"They did; I took one of their hands," she replied, with a slight smile. The stranger started to laugh.

"Good, those bastards need to be taken down a notch." A smile ran across Oranna's lips, and she knew she was strong.

"My name is Oranna. What do they call you?"

"Me? Well, many things: lover, thief, scholar, rogue, handsome," he joked.

"Your name, boy, not your titles!" she snapped.

"Alright, alright, where I'm from they call me Orthindu."

"And where do you come from?" Oranna asked curiously.

"The Land of Lakes. My town was attacked. Mostly older fishermen and families lived there. They slaughtered most of them. The ones who could fight, they kept. But I'm the only one left."

"What happened to the others?"

"Sport for the creatures. They'd unlock a cage, someone would 'escape,' and the creatures would hunt them down."

"Why did they not get you?"

"Because when my turn came, I didn't leave."

"You can add coward to your 'titles'," she retorted.

"Well, forgive me for not wanting to die for nothing." Orthindu turned away, and they rode in silence.

A few hours passed, and the caravan stopped for the night. The raiders built a fire and began drinking and feasting. As Oranna looked around, she noticed that they didn't seem to be very alert. No one was keeping watch, and no one was armed. She looked over at Orthindu. He was staring into the fire, seemingly hypnotized by the flames. Oranna kicked his foot, startling him.

"What do you want?" he growled.

"Look, they're all distracted or passed out," she replied. Orthindu scanned the raiders. "Your point?"

"We can escape. We can slay them and be on our way?" she said.

Orthindu burst into laughter. "This isn't funny," she said sternly. His laughter was loud, and a raider threw a cup at the cage, making a loud crash.

"Keep it down, slave," the raider shouted. Orthindu quieted down but kept smiling. "What is so funny?" she asked.

"The cages are unlocked, and the raiders are drunk, but the creatures lie in wait for a dumb soul like yourself to devour," he replied. Oranna looked out into the night but didn't see anyone or anything.

"Where are they?" she asked.

"Trees, probably," Orthindu shook his head and ran his hands through his hair. "Best not to think about it," he said. With that, he rolled over and stared into the fire. Oranna couldn't help but stare into the nothingness that is the night, trying to spot them. Yet, she saw nothing.

Late in the evening, after the fire had died out, Oranna was stirred awake by a sound. As she slowly rose and looked around, she noticed that one of the captives had figured out that the cages were unlocked. Oranna held her breath and watched as he opened the cage and cautiously stepped out.

He took a few steps and stopped, as if he had heard something. He looked around and was suddenly overtaken by the creatures. Oranna looked on in horror as the camp was filled with his screams. The raiders awoke and laughed as they watched the creatures tear him apart.

Oranna's gaze was then met by a creature that dropped in front of her, baring its teeth. As she stared it down, she noticed that it was missing a hand. She stepped closer and could feel its hot, foul breath stinging her nostrils. "You want to lose more than just your hand?" she smirked. In an instant, its remaining hand shot through the bars and grabbed her. However, she was swift and countered by grabbing its wrist. With a quick twist, she broke the creature's wrist and pulled it close. As it howled in pain, she seized its throat and squeezed. The raiders rushed over, and the other creatures turned to see. Despite the raiders' efforts, they couldn't pry Oranna's hand from the creature's throat. It squirmed and squealed until Oranna crushed its windpipe.

Oranna stepped back as the creature's lifeless body crumbled to the ground. The raiders stepped back in fear and exchanged worried glances. The remaining creatures emitted a gruesome moan at the sight of their brother being killed. The raiders locked Oranna's cage, and for the rest of the night, they kept a watchful eye on her.

Oranna sat staring at the raiders until the first light of morning. Orthindu awoke and sleepily looked around. "What happened last night?" he asked. "Hey, what happened?" He threw hay at her. Without breaking eye contact, she replied, "I killed a creature last night by crushing its throat." A look of disbelief washed over Orthindu's face.

"You did what?"

"The creature tried to grab me, so I broke its wrist and strangled it," she said. Orthindu looked at her with astonishment and fear in his eyes. He scooted closer and whispered, "In all the raids I've been dragged to, no one has ever once harmed the creatures, let alone killed one. You are truly great. And I think with your help, we could escape." Oranna turned and glared at him. Orthindu sheepishly smiled and backed away.

"Now you talk of escape? Once you know how strong I am, you want my help. Why?" she demanded.

"Because I was scared before, but now I think we could do this," he said.

"We?!" she scoffed. "You mean me," Orthindu nodded his head in shame. "I will be escaping tonight. If you wish to come with me, know this: if you slow me down or put yourself before others, I will slice you in half." Frightened, he extended his hand. "Agreed."

The raiders packed up camp and headed to their next target. Late in the day, a scout rode up and informed them of a small village up ahead. After a few exchanged words, they quickened their pace. They left the wagons on the outskirts of the village and commenced their attack. Oranna realized that this was the perfect opportunity to escape. She woke up Orthindu. "I need you to pick the lock," she said.

"What makes you think I have that skill?" he asked.

"Do you?" she snapped.

"Of course, but it hurts that you would just assume I know how," he said. Oranna rolled her eyes and shoved Orthindu towards the lock. In only a few seconds, the cage was open, and they stepped out.

She rushed over to the other wagons to search for her gear. "Can you help me find my things?" Oranna turned and saw Orthindu running into the forest. "Damn him!" She continued to search and found her urgrosh and some supplies. Oranna ran over to the other cages and attempted to free the captives.

She broke the lock, and the people stepped back in fear. Slowly, Oranna turned to find that one of the creatures was standing behind her. She evaluated it and assumed a fighting stance. The creature threw off its tattered robe, revealing its body. It stood nearly 6.5 feet tall, hunched over. Its arms were long and ended in razor-like claws. The creature snarled, showing its needle-like teeth, then lunged at Oranna with a roar.

Oranna blocked the first strike and evaded the next. She rolled to the right, but the creature was quick. It grabbed her by the waist and threw her as if she weighed nothing. Oranna hit the ground and sprang back to her feet, ready to continue the fight. The creature snarled, and slobber dripped from its chin as it advanced on her. Oranna sidestepped each of its attacks and countered with her own, slashing its leg, ribs, and back. But nothing seemed to slow it down. Her strength was waning quickly.

Just as the creature was about to strike again, the sound of a horse caught its attention. Orthindu rode up, sword drawn, and crashed down on the creature's skull. They both fell to the ground. Orthindu struggled to retrieve his sword, for it was stuck. He hurried over to Oranna and assisted her onto the horse. As he mounted the horse, behind them, a group of raiders galloped back into camp. With an arrow notched, a raider let it fly. Oranna watched in slow motion as the arrow pierced Orthindu's back. He exhaled a rush of blood and slumped over. She urged the horse to go faster and disappeared into the forest.

The raiders tossed their new captives into cages, and the third creature entered into camp. It saw its deceased brother and turned to the raider captain. It seized the captain's throat, and raised him in the air. Through clenched teeth the captain whispered, "I...release you...go and hunt." In a flash, the creature vanished, hot on their trail.

    Oranna and Orthindu rode hard and fast through the forest until she spotted a small cave. She dragged Orthindu inside and quickly unloaded the supplies from the horse, sending it off into the forest. In the cave, she propped Orthindu up against the wall, blood seeping through his shirt.

    "That was foolish of you," Oranna remarked as she tended to his wounds.

    "I couldn't leave a damsel in distress like you," he replied. "I was going to leave, but I couldn't live knowing you might be dead," he continued. "When you called me a coward, it made me reflect on my life and how I've run from many hardships. When they captured me, I wasn't defending the village, I was running to escape. That's how they found me."

Oranna saw that he was telling the truth. "One good deed cannot absolve you of all your wrongs. But it's a start," she stated.

"Thanks. Now, can you remove this arrow?" Orthindu asked.

"Already done," Oranna responded, dropping the arrow in front of him. She finished binding Orthindu's wound and made a bed for him to rest.

"What now?" he asked.

She looked at him and replied, "We wait." As she turned, Orthindu passed out from exhaustion and drifted into a deep sleep.

Throughout the night, the forest came to life with the music of owls, crickets, and the gentle rustling of the trees. The fireflies lit the darkness, and the stars sparkled above. Yet, Oranna couldn't shake the sensation that she was being watched. Ever vigilant, she stood guard till morning.

As the sun rose, Orthindu stirred. "We're going to free the others," Oranna declared. He rolled over and looked at her in disbelief, "Are you feeling okay?"

"Yes," Oranna replied.

Orthindu looked at her, "I know whatever you're planning will lead to victory." He laughed and she returned a smile, saying, "Get dressed, we leave soon."

Once dressed, they set off east. "How do you know they went this way?" Orthindu inquired. Oranna pointed to the sky behind her, "See, there's a large amount of smoke. That's the village they attacked." She then pointed east, saying, " A small column of smoke means the caravan went this way." Orthindu nodded, and they followed the trail of smoke.

When they arrived, the campsite was deserted. There were tracks leading east, but Oranna noticed tracks around the campsite. "They freed the creature," she said.

"How do you know that?" Orthindu asked.

"See here," she explained, "they had men standing guard at each wagon. That means the creature is what I felt last night."

"Felt last night?! What does that mean?" Orthindu asked.

"We're being hunted. We must move quickly," she replied and they started running after the caravan.

After an hour of tracking, the caravan could be heard clanking along. Oranna stopped and waited for Orthindu to catch up. Once he caught up, they laid out their plan of attack.

The caravan was moving slowly with supplies and new captives in their cages. The captain was nervous as he no longer had his creatures to protect them and had to rely solely on his men. A scream filled the air, and upon investigation, they found that the rear guard was dead. Another scream followed, and the guard at the front was found dead without his head. "Spread out and take up arms. The creature has returned," the captain commanded. The raiders drew their swords and prepared for a fight.

"I am no creature," a voice echoed through the trees. The raiders looked around but saw no one. "I will be the last face you see on this earth," the voice continued. Another raider collapsed dead.

"Show yourself so it may be a fair fight," the captain shouted fearfully.

"As fair as you were when you raided a village," the voice retorted. The captain scoffed, but as he turned, another of his men lay dead.

"I will have your head!" he yelled. In that instant, Oranna dropped behind him, she wrapped her hand around his neck, and whispered, "Not if I take yours first." She swiftly drew her blade across his throat, and held his severed head in her hand. His men stared in horror.

"If you value your lives, run!" The raiders scattered like roaches, disappearing into the forest. As Oranna climbed down from the wagon, she heard a screech and a roar, knowing the creature was next to face its fate.

"Orthindu, hurry and free the others. I'll deal with it." Oranna commanded. Orthindu peeked out from under a wagon and nodded. Oranna stood ready as the shadowy creature emerged at the top of the hill, roaring to the heavens. "Bring your filth here to meet my blade," she taunted. It came down on all fours, sending leaves and dirt flying behind it as its claws dug into the earth, rushing towards her. Just before it struck, she leaped, and it slammed into the wagon. Oranna vaulted over it and drove her urgrosh into its back.

She landed on her feet and swiftly turned. The creature stood, cracked its neck, and faced her. Without a moment's hesitation, she struck its neck, but to her surprise, it grabbed the urgrosh and wrenched it from Oranna's grip. She stumbled back, reaching for her blade, but stumbled as she retreated.

Oranna threw the blade as she fell, striking the creature in the chest, but it continued its relentless assault.

It raised its hand, poised to strike her down. Oranna let out a warrior's cry. The creature laughed and raised its hands higher to strike. She closed her eyes and heard the sound of its claws piercing flesh and felt blood, but no pain. When she opened her eyes, she saw that its claws had pierced Orthindu. The creature was as surprised as she was. She rolled away and kicked the creature's knee. Oranna grabbed the hilt of the blade sticking out of its chest and pushed it deeper. The creature wailed in pain. She stepped back and picked up her urgrosh. Never breaking eye contact, Oranna sliced through the air and its head left its shoulders as its lifeless body crumbled to the ground.

She turned to see Orthindu lying in a pool of blood. Oranna rushed to his side, propping him up against a tree. Placing her hands on his face. "Did you stop it?"

"Yes, we stopped it," she assured him, her voice quivered as she fought back tears.

"Good. Just so you know, that's the last time I save you." Orthindu chuckled weakly, his laughter giving way to groans.

"Why did you do that?" she inquired, locking her eyes on him searching for an explanation.

"From the moment I saw you, I knew you'd be a hero. You slew the creatures, you saved me, and you freed them. Thanks for letting me save you." Orthindu murmured with his fading final breath. Oranna's tears flowed softly as kissed his forehead.

As the sun set, Oranna completed the solemn task burying Orthindu. The people she had freed stood around to pay their respects. In the gathering, a small girl approached her and gently placed an amulet and a note into her hand.

As the wagons were being packed, Oranna read the note: "*Oranna, if you're reading this, then I picked the right person to give it to and I'm dead. I haven't known you long, but I know a hero when I see one. This was the amulet of the Lakes, passed down from king to king. I won't say how I got it, but know it wasn't easy. You've been more of a friend to me than anyone I have ever known. So please wear it with the honor I never did. I don't want to say I love you, but I think you know the truth. Take care. You are a real hero in this world of evil, and it needs you.*"

Oranna wiped the tears from her eyes and gazed ahead with hope as the last rays of the sun vanished on the horizon. She smiled, knowing many more adventures lay before her. Oranna, the Slayer of Demons, bearer of the Amulet of Lakes, friend and lover of Orthindu.

River Gale

Its mighty and strong
The river running long

Flowing deep and wide
I dare not ride

From mountains it comes
To the sea it goes

Through valley and dale
Shall ever flow the river gale

Found at the Ruins of Orasul
Unknown Soldier's Journal

The Rescue of Princess Bajaw

The tavern door swung open, and a cold wind rushed in. Two imperial guards in full armor crossed the threshold. All eyes were fixed on the door.

"His Royal Highness King Louk is looking for adventures. If you come with us, you will be rewarded."

The tavern's patrons looked around. Most of them were simple farmers or herdsmen, not warriors. "Is there anyone willing?" Once again, the room was silent. The guards scanned the room and pointed, "You there, in the corner, are you not an adventurer?" All eyes in the room turned to see who was in the corner.

In the corner sat Oranna, a barbarian from the northern mountain tribe. Clad in studded leather armor, she drinks from her stein. Peering over the rim, her hazel eyes pierce the very souls of the guards, causing them to shudder. She finished her drink, stood up, grabbed her urgrosh from the corner and walked to the door.

Gazing out into the cold night, she looks over her shoulder. "Well are you coming, or should I walk myself to the palace?" With that said, she and the guards headed to meet with the king.

Coming from the Northern Mountains, the idea of having a king was foreign to her. She had grown up under a clan leader. Whenever issues within the land, the other clan leaders would convene and form a war council. There was no single ruler.

As the throne room doors creaked opened, she was surprised to see King Louk seated on the throne. Here seated in a jewel encrusted throne sat a stout, portly man. Contrary to the image of a king, he appeared dirty with flies buzzing around the half eaten plates about his throne. A king should be fierce and strong, but this king was very soft and not terrifying at all. The Clan leader was a formidable warrior that led with strength but also wisdom. Her mind wondered why he was chosen king.

    She approached the throne and the king's plump hand gestured for her to stop. One of the guards stepped forth, "Your Royal Highness, may I introduce you to Oranna of the North." The king's gaze swept her over. "A woman? Were there no strong men that would come to my aid in my hour of darkness?" Flecks of spittle sprayed from his mouth as he talked. Oranna let out an audible sigh and shot a glare at the king. He continued, "I needed a warrior and you bring me a handmaiden in armor. Please go back and find..." Before he could finish, a dagger whizzed past his head, striking a fly out of the air. The king clutched his chest and fell back. The guards turned their attention and quickly rushed her. Oranna spun and knocked the guards into each other. With a devilish grin and her hands in her hips, she planted a foot on one of them, pinning him down. Her gaze pierced the king, "I'm very tough and can handle anything. Now tell me how I can help."

King Louk, still sweating, stammered, "a group of mercenaries known as the Ravagers kidnapped my daughter while she was out riding. I would like to hire you to rescue her." Oranna walked up to the king, leaned in, retrieved her knife from the throne, "If I do this, will you reward me?" The King nodded. Oranna straightened up, resheathed her knife and accepted the terms.

The princess had gone for a ride through the valley and into the Crested Forest and didn't return. Before the sun's first light had brushed the castle wall, Oranna set out from the southern gate to track down and rescue the princess. She rode past small farms and houses on her way to the forest. Villagers stared as she rode through town. It was very unusual to see someone from the mountains this far south, let alone a woman, especially riding a wolf. She brushed off their stares and gawks and pressed on.

    Right before you enter the Crested Forest, there stands a stone bridge, said to have been built by the first settlers, spanning the Gale river. Oranna dismounted and walked across, struck by the beauty of the masonary work, as well as the scenery. Behind her to the north, the sprawling city with its high towers and banners waving in the wind. Beyond lay the mountains of her home. To the east, the river flowed fast, winding back and forth, weaving its way across the land. To the west, stretched the open plains and hills of Fathom, rumored to be rich with both treasure and danger. And to the south waited the Crested Forest, its thick wood was alive with the changing.

Colors of yellow, red, and orange painted the forest. The wind gently sent the scents of autumn dancing through the air. As Oranna breathed the crisp morning air her riding wolf, Ymora, began to whine. Oranna spun around, to see, at the end of the bridge stood two large men.

The men barring the path were draped in several layers of furs and tattered rags, their odor was of blood and filth. Each of them had a serrated dagger drawn. The taller of the two had a slacked expression, while the smaller one had a scar across his scalp.

"Let me pass," Oranna commanded. The brutes looked at each other, "No," said the scarred one. Oranna scowled at them, "Why?"

"Dis here bridge is the passage into the realm of da ravagers. And you must pay da toll," the small brute explained.

Standing with arms crossed and chest out, Oranna spoke, "What is the price?"

"Simple," the small brute continued. "A, you gives us all ya supplies or 2, you pay with blood and we take your supplies." The brutes smiled, revealing mouths full of rotten and broken teeth.

Oranna stared at each of them. "Here's what's going to happen. I'm going to whistle, and my wolf will tear your face off, little one. It will be so shocking that your big friend won't know what to do but look in horror, I'll run up and take out his knees, as he falls to the ground, I'll hit the rest of his teeth out. And while you both lay on the ground bleeding, I'll end your miserable lives with my urgrosh."

The brutes burst into laughter. "Little ting like you goin to all dat."

Oranna smirked and nodded. "Or you can tell me where Princess Bajaw is and live the rest of your lives out?"

"Da pretty lady at da fortress?" Said the ugly brute. He quickly placed a hand over his mouth as his friend glared at him.

Before they could reconsider, Oranna whistled, and Ymora lunged into action, taking down the scarred brute. The ugly brute froze in horror, looking on in bewilderment. A sharp pain jolted through his right knee, causing him to collapse. As he fell, he caught the hardest fist he'd ever felt, leaving his mouth filled with blood and bits of teeth. Oranna whistled once more and Ymora released her jaw from the scarred brute's face. She drew her urgrosh and with two slashes they were both gone.

    Oranna tended to Ymora, cleaning her up, and gathered supplies from the duo and headed off to the fortress of the Ravagers. As she searched the woods, the scent of fires and the distant clamor of the fort could be heard. She knew that the main path would be heavily guarded, and although she could take them head on, she didn't want to waste an entire day fighting.

    In the heart of the Crested Forest there was a natural spring, its waters formed a small tributary into the Gale river. Oranna knew that this was the Ravagers source of water, and it would be an easy way to infiltrate the fort. She navigated the rugged terrain of the woods, Oranna had unhooked Ymora and let her run freely. The wolf darted back and forth, making wide circles, she was truly at home in the woods. Keeping pace with Ymora, they located the spring. Oranna looked at Ymora and scratched her chin, around her cheek, and up behind the ear. Ymora nuzzled her head into Orannas hand. "Good girl, now I need you to wait here until I return." Oranna instructed. Ymora looked at her, head cocked. Oranna looked lovingly into her eyes, she had raised Ymora from a pup. Ymora licked her face and darted off into the trees. "Stay safe." As Ymora disappeared into the trees. As night's shadows lengthened, Oranna plunged into the spring.

  The Ravagers had rerouted the spring so it flowed through their fort. The spring entered through a small grated hole in the side of the fort. Wading up to the grate, Oranna noticed it was loosely held together by ropes. She placed a hand on either side, she attempted to pull it off. However, the grate didn't budge. She tightened her grip and pulled harder. Yet, again the grate remained unmoved. Determined, Oranna bent down and summoned every muscle in her body. She could feel the ache in her arms and back. Her jaw clenched, and with one more pull, the grate snapped. Oranna fell backward into the water, gasping for a deep breath. As she sat up, she could now easily access the fort with a bit of stealth. The intake was small and she had to crawl through.

    The spring ran under the dining hall and into the courtyard. Peering up through the cracks in the floor, Oranna could see several people eating and drinking. She tried to eavesdrop, in hopes of finding the location of the Princess, but she heard no mention. At the opening where the spring emerged, she had a view of the entire courtyard. To the north stood the front gate, guarded by four spearmen. To the left of the gate was the stable that had several horses, to the right of the gate was the blacksmith's smelter and anvil, with someone still working. On the eastern wall, the barracks were visible, as several men had gone inside. Positioned on the southern wall was the dining hall, while the grand hall occupied the western wall.

    She knew that the barracks would be full of Ravagers sleeping, and before long, those in the dining hall would join them. If she waited patiently, they would all be passed out from eating and drinking. That would be her opportunity for her to slip into the grand hall to see if the Princess was there.

    The moon rose, but offered little light to her advantage. After an hour passed, the dining hall was cleared, and the roaring fires became smoldering embers. Oranna emerged from the shadows, She crept along the side of the wall, dodging drunks, and torches light. Eventually, she reached a side hatch of the grand hall and skillfully pried it open.

The hatch opened to a set of stone steps leading into a darkened cellar. Oranna carefully shuffled down the steps, ensuring she made no sound until she made it to the dirt floor. As her eyes adjusted to the dim light, she could make out the storeroom. Massive barrels of beer lined the walls, and shelves held other supplies of flour, salt and cooking ingredients.

She made her way to the stairs and cautiously crept up them, until she entered the grand hall. She entered a large stone throne room, on the back wall was an intricately carved wooden throne. A fire pit warmed the hall in the middle of the room. To the right, a staircase led up to the second floor and two guards slept at their post. Her gaze swept the room, there behind the throne was a large tattered tapestry. With careful steps she made her way over, and began to climb until she reached the rafters of the hall. The largest cross beam spanned the entire hall, connecting to the upper level. Slowly, she moved across the beam with exceptional balance, and hopped onto the second level.

    The second level was a long stone hallway that led to a single wooden door. As Oranna approached the door cautiously, the soft cries of a woman could be heard. Oranna quickly reached for the handle and noticed it wasn't locked. Taking a deep breath, she burst through the door, urgrosh drawn, prepared to fight. However, she wasn't expecting to see a beautiful woman with golden hair, wrapped in the arms of an equally beautiful man. Confused, she couldn't help but stare.

    Within a few seconds, the lovers realized they were not alone. The woman let out a piercing scream and quickly rolled off her lover, covering her nakedness with blankets. In a fury, the man stumbled out of bed and drew his dagger.

"Come no closer, assassin, if you value your life," the young man shouted, quivering. Oranna shut and locked the door and placed her hands on her hips, "I've come for the girl."

The man glanced down at the naked woman, then at the door and back at Oranna. "Take her if you must, but my men will come for you. For our love cannot be separated."

A scoff came from the woman, "You would just let an assassin take me? And then send your men to find me? I thought you loved me!" The man looked at her and shrugged.

Oranna laughed. "So let me get this straight: the handsome man is the leader of the dirty Ravagers. You are Princess Bajaw. You two have fallen in love and taken up residence here, which I'm guessing is owned by your father," she motioned toward the man. "Who is the king of Eastmarch based on the sigil? Your father," Oranna pointed at Princess Bajaw, "King Louk of Norden, didn't want you two to marry so you ran off. Is that correct?" The two nod their heads.

"I see," Oranna pondered for a moment. "Well, your father hired me to rescue you, and considering how easily he gave you up, I am willing to bet you'll come." Princess Bajaw nodded her head. "Go dress, and we shall leave." Princess Bajaw hurried into another room to get dressed.

Oranna walked over to the Prince of Eastmarch and looked him up and down. "A bit chilly tonight?" she asked with a playful smile. He quickly covered himself, blushing from embarrassment. "If you ever "fall in love" again, you must be willing to give your life for her, or you will never truly be a man."

The Prince sat down and started to cry. He spoke through tears, " I am a man, and I do love her, and I won't let you stop me." With that, he rose with a dagger in hand, ready to strike. Oranna grabbed his wrist and squeezed, causing him to drop the dagger. She tightened her grip, dropping him to his knees, and with a swift punch he crumpled to the floor. Just then Princess Bajaw opened the door and stepped out.

"What has happened to him?" Princess Bajaw inquired, with little concern in her voice. "He passed out. Are you ready?" Oranna asked. She nodded and the two left the room, and continued down the hall toward the crossbeam. Oranna jumped up to cross it, and Princess Bajaw puzzled, questioned, "What are you doing? Are you mad?"

"There are two guards at the bottom of the stairs. We need to sneak past them," Oranna explained.

"Don't worry; they all love me here. I'm basically their mother," Princess Bajaw replied with a grin and confidently went down the stairs. Oranna followed quickly and the two walked past the guards.

As they opened the hall door and stepped into the night, Orannas confidence in escaping without incident grew. The pair hurried across the courtyard towards the stables. However, before they could mount their escape, they heard the Prince of Eastmarch's voice, "Stop them! An assassin is stealing my beloved!" The two exited the stable to see the courtyard was now full of ravagers.

"Prepare the horses." Oranna instructed calmly.

"Don't hurt them," Princess Bajaw replied.

Oranna turned and glared. Bajaw stepped back into the stable, understanding the unspoken command, and began to prepare the horses.

Oranna let out a heavy sigh, drew her urgrosh, and stepped to the center of the courtyard, and took a fighting stance. The Prince marched up to her, anger clung to his words, "You trash barbarian! Do you think you can steal my destiny away from me? My men will rip you to pieces. And I will become the king of both Eastmarch and Norden."

A smirk ran across Oranna's face, "The only trash here is you." With a wink she front kicked the Prince into the mud. Without hesitation, she charged the Ravagers.

The battle began with Oranna sweeping her urgrosh neck height, smacking several rushing men into the mud. A sword slashed past her face, and she dodged, countering with a punch that knocked him out. She spun around and blocked an axe coming down, then pushed her assailant back, knocking him off balance. A spearman charged at her, with her urgrosh, she deflected the spear up and over her shoulder, she then punched the spearman in the stomach. As he fell, two arms grabbed her from behind and lifted her into the air. Seizing the opportunity, several more rushed in. Oranna rolled forward with all her might, flinging the assailant into his comrades. Causing them to crash into the mud.

As she glared into the eyes of the Ravagers, an arrow narrowly missed her left ear. She turned, only to be caught by a second arrow through her thigh. She fell to a knee. Before the next arrow could be loosed, her dagger twirled through the air and struck the archer in the shoulder. Ignoring the pain, she rose with the arrow still lodged in her leg and assessed her surroundings. The Ravagers, swords drawn, closed in around her. With a barbarian cry, Oranna charged forward. Just then the nick of time, Princess Bajaw, on horseback, leaped in between them and Oranna. The princess quickly dismounted and unsheathed her own sword. With a few slashes and thrusts in the air the Ravagers backed away.

A dozen Ravagers lay moaning in the courtyard. Princess Bajaw extended her hand and helped Oranna to her feet. The Prince yelled, "Kill them, don't stop, kill them!" But the Ravagers remained still. "Why won't you idiots listen!"

"You never respected them; I treated them like people, not animals." The Princess replied firmly. "I don't love this Prince anymore. Please, let me and my friend pass peacefully, or we will have to fight our way out." The Ravagers exchanged glances, and stepped to the side.

"What are you doing? Stop her!" Screamed the Prince. Princess Bajaw helped Oranna onto a horse, and the two made their way towards the gate. As the heavy doors creaked open the Prince raised a spear and took aim. Just before he could release it, a blood curdling howl echoed behind him. Everyone turned, just in time to witness Ymora leaping through the air, her mouth open and teeth gleaming in the torch light. Her teeth met the Prince with a bone chilling scream, and with a fierce shake the Prince was back in the mud, bleeding. Oranna whistled, and

Ymora released her grip on the Prince's shoulder. She pranced to the side of Oranna, and together, the threesome left the fort.

They all made it to the bridge just as the first light of sunrise brushed the land. They stood in silence, watching as the morning sun warmed them. "Thank you, for saving me." Princess Bajaw finally spoke. "It was my honor," Oranna smiled with a hint of pride.

"I'll be sure to have my father pay you well." Princess Bajaw said petting Ymora.

"I've never had a friend before and I'd like to think we are friends." Oranna smiled and pulled out her drinking horn. She took a long slow drink and passed it over.

"I don't have many friends either, so I'm proud to call *you* friend." Laughter filled the air, as the two friends shared the horn, passing it back and forth.

They mounted up and returned to the Kingdom of Norden. Oranna was rewarded with treasure and the title of Protector. She stayed for a while healing her wound and strengthening the bonds of friendship. The day Oranna left she knew that even though she wasn't born here she could call this place home.

Voyage to the Isle of Forgotten

The Diamond Sea is said to have no end. Sailors tell tales of shadows and foul creatures lurking beyond the horizon. However, for Oranna, the water had always been a source of tranquility. Often, she would sit on the docks that grace the harbor of Eastmarch, contemplating life's great questions. Her thoughts often wandered toward adventure on the waves, the treasures of mysterious lands, and one day, leading her own crew of fearless warriors to battle on those distant shores.

Today, her dream had become a reality. She had enlisted to be part of a crew bound for the islands of Costa del Sol, rumored to be filled with untold treasures.

She tossed her bag onto the deck and leaped aboard. As she scanned the upper deck, the rest of the crew just stared unblinking at her. It seemed they had never encountered a woman on board a ship before. Oranna collected her gear and made her way towards the crew's quarters. A tall, rugged man barred the doorway. "Crew members only," he grumbled. Oranna simply looked at him. They locked eyes, staring at each other, slowly he began to reach for his dagger. Before he could unsheathe it, in the blink of an eye, Oranna drew a short sword and held it against his throat.

    The rest of the crew gathered around, tension hung in the air. "I wouldn't do that," a voice called from above. All eyes left the situation and shifted to the bridge, except for Oranna; her gaze remained fixed on her target. The owner of the voice descended the steps and stood before her. "Look, I get it, Jamison's an ass, in both looks and smell," the crew chuckled, "but he's also one of the strongest sailors I know." Oranna's nostrils flared. "Plus, down there is where all the smelly boys sleep. I've arranged a cabin just for you." Oranna finally broke her gaze, turning to see the intervening voice.

There stood a man at an average height and build, his skin was kissed by the sun to a perfect bronze hue. His dark, wavy hair and beard bore traces of sweat and salt, yet still appeared cleaner than half of the others. His eyes held a kind, but weathered, expression, as if he had known great loss. He extended his hand. "Please, come with me." As swiftly as she had drawn her sword, Oranna resheathed it and she stepped back.

She followed him through a door, past the galley, and into a back room. The man unlocked the door, pushed it open, and she stepped inside. The room featured a small bed tucked into the corner, a window offering a glimpse of the outside world, a bookshelf filled with books and maps, and even a small table with four chairs. In a cupboard, there were several plates, cups and bottles of wine. She turned to see the man smiling. "It's all yours. Make yourself comfortable, and when you're ready, head up top; the captain will be casting off soon."

    Oranna inspected the room and stowed her belongings. She checked the bookshelf and found a map of Costa del Sol. Her eyes traced the lines on the map, as they passed over several uncharted areas around the islands. She noticed a particular section of the map had been circled. It appeared to be a location entirely off the map. The sight of the map filled her with uneasiness regarding the journey, but she knew she was prepared for the unknown.

    Oranna made her way to the deck just as the ship was venturing into open water. As she stepped through the doorway, a small bearded man handed her a mop and bucket. "You're swabbing the deck. Gotta keep it dry," he said with a mischievous grin. Several crew members chuckled as Oranna glared at them.

Without complaint, she worked hard, offering to lend a hand wherever she could to help. After midday, the cook made the rounds with food for the crew. Everyone received a slice of bread, an orange, and a chunk of dried meat. But when the cook reached Oranna, she peered into the basket and found it empty. The cook shrugged and remarked, "I'll make more for dinner," before he hobbled back to the kitchen.

Oranna leaned over the railing, gazing at the land that was shrinking in the distance. The water lapped at the side of the ship as it crashed from one wave to the next. A smile crept across Oranna's face as flying fish leaped at the bow.

"Heads up," a voice called, and without even looking, Oranna caught an orange from the air.

"Nice catch," It was the man from earlier.

"Enjoying your time?" Her gaze fixed on

the waves.

"It's not what I thought it would be." Oranna said in a solemn voice.

"Ah, she does speak," he said, hopping on the railing. She glanced at him and rolled her eyes. "Well it may not be the nicest crew or exactly as you thought, but give it a chance and shape it into what you want."

With that, he finished speaking and flipped over the side.

Oranna stepped back, her eyes widening as the man fell. But surprise quickly turned to amusement as the man grabbed a rope as he fell, swinging down and dragging his feet in the water before swinging back on deck. Standing in amazement, he sauntered over and handed her the rope.

"Go on, it's a right of passage for each new crew member."

Oranna never backed down, grabbed the rope, and stepped onto the railing. With a deep breath, she jumped. The fall was exhilarating, and the tension in the rope as it swung her near the waves was almost spiritual. She moved quickly as the spray of the sea kissed her face. She laughed as she swung back on the deck. Most of the crew cheered as she successfully stuck her landing. They gathered around her and welcomed her into the crew.

    The day stretched on, with tasks completed as the sun's last rays danced on the horizon, painting the sky shades of pink and purple. The cook shuffled about, serving a meal to everyone. Some dined in the galley, while others gathered in small groups around the deck. Music and merriment filled the ship. Oranna settled down by one of the fire braziers with a few fellow crew members. She listened intently as they shared tales of far off lands, wars, and adventures. As they ate, she noticed the man wandering about, conversing with the crew but never pausing for more than a few laughs.

"Who is he?" she finally asked. A one-eyed sailor turned to see, and chuckled to himself. "Aye, that be the captain, Captain Maso."

Surprised, Oranna nearly choked on her meal. "The captain? But he seems so… young."

"Aye, one of the youngest," the sailor confirmed. "He got the rank of captain during the great war. He served as a cabin boy on a ship that engaged the enemy. Cannons and arrows filled the air, bodies piled knee high, and the cursed dwarves set their own ship ablaze, aiming to ram the fleet. Maso clutched the helm and steered it clear of the dwarves' vessel. But the ordeal wasn't over. As the ship burned, the flames reached the gunpowder stores and exploded , raining fire down on the fleet. Maso steered the burning wreck into the shallows, attempting to save as many lives as possible. But their own powder ignited, and it detonated before he could get everyone off. He was thrown by the blast into the water with twenty others, yet when they were finally rescued, only eleven remained and among the dead was his own brother. Word of his heroic deeds eventually reached the king, and once the war concluded, they appointed him captain and gave him command of this ship. Now, he sails, charting courses for merchants and discovering new routes."

Oranna sat in amazement. Her thoughts turned to her own loss of friends as she caressed the amulet around her neck.

For the next few days, it was the same routine, day in and day out. They cleaned, they ate, they worked, they played, they ate again. One evening, about a week after they set out, Oranna approached the Captain.

"That's your room correct?" Oranna asked.

Without looking up, the Captain replied, "It was, but now it's yours."

"Why?" she remarked.

"Some sailors have superstitions about a woman on a ship. Now, I don't care, as long as you work, that's fine." Oranna listened intently. "But I don't want my crew to have issues. Cause when it comes down to it, you need to count on each other." The Captain looked up and into her eyes.

"Can I count on you?" As she looked into his eyes, she could see his kindness but also his command and passion. Oranna nodded. He smiled and winked. "I knew I could."

Oranna went back to work the next morning before dawn. The watch rotation had fallen on her, and she climbed the mast to take her seat. At the top of the mast, you could see for miles all around. It was beautiful watching the sunrise here. As she gazed out, she saw a huge black shadow forming. She called down, "Storm six miles out, forming off the port bow side." The Captain held his hand to his brow. The storm was large and moving fast. Flashes of lightning could be seen, and claps of thunder rolled over the open water. "Prepare to get wet boys." With that, the crew jumped into action as the storm fell upon them.

    An hour into the storm, and the ship was enveloped in darkness. They had already lost a few men as waves swept over the deck. The wind was so strong it tore through the mainsail. The wind and waves battered the ship. With all hands on deck, Oranna had come down to help keep things tied down. As they worked, a bolt of lightning struck the mast. It cracked and buckled and began to fall. The mast crashed onto the deck, boards splintering and ropes flying. The ship seemed doomed. A cry from the bow, "ROCKS!" The captain spun the helm, but the keel crashed against the rocks. Water began rushing into the ship. There was creaking and cracking of planks as the waves pushed the ship into the rocks.

    The Captain cried out, " Abandon ship!" The crew looked back and heard the pain in his voice. "Boys, she won't hold; we have to save ourselves." With that, the men headed towards the lifeboats. As the crew members rushed, Oranna heard another cry. Looking down, she saw Jamison trapped under the mast, looking pitiful and helpless. Without hesitation or thought of her own life, she reached down and wrapped her arms around the mast. Using all her strength, she began to lift the mast. Her legs began to burn, and her heart raced in her chest. The mast budged, and she let out a savage roar as it rose just enough for him to escape.

    Once free, Oranna dropped the mast and helped Jamison up. They shuffled over to the railing as the last lifeboat was lowered into the water. Oranna looked at him and said, "Right of passage?" He nodded. Oranna grabbed a rope, held tight, and swung down: plummeting, the yardarm gave way, and they both plunged into the water.

Oranna had a difficult time treading the rough water. The lifeboat was still a ways away. As they got closer, Oranna tried to climb aboard but slipped back into the water. She felt a hand hoist her up. Looking back, she saw Jamison lifting her. She toppled into the boat just as a wave swept him into the jagged rocks. Oranna fell to the floor, gasping for air, and those remaining in the boat tried their best to keep them alive. A massive wave sailed them perilously close to the rocks. With another wave, the boat capsized, and everything went dark.

    Coughing and choking, Oranna opened her eyes. She was unaware of her surroundings; all she knew was her body ached. It felt like she had been punched by the Giants of Cloud Mountain. She rolled over, feeling the sand and rocks between her fingers, and looked up to the blinding sun. She slowly sat up and scanned her surroundings. She found herself on an empty beach, covered by wreckage.

She tried to stand, but a sharp pain shot through her side. Looking down, she saw a sizable gash, bloody and wet. Her shoulder throbbed with pain, and as she touched it, she knew it had been dislocated. Gritting her teeth, she took a deep breath and reset her shoulder with a pop and scream.

Oranna walked the beach, searching the wreckage for survivors and supplies. She found some herbs and somewhat clean cloth to bind her wounds. As she continued, she was startled to find a horse tangled in ropes. She approached it with careful consideration. "Shh... easy," she said softly. Kneeling, she gently rubbed the horse. To her surprise, the horse had no injuries. Oranna freed the horse, and it stood with great force, shaking off the sand. Oranna stepped back, not wanting to get trampled, but the horse looked at her calmly, bobbing its head, as if to say thank you. Oranna extended a steady hand, and the horse met her. She stared into its eyes, and it nayed and nodded. Oranna mounted the horse and headed down the beach for anyone at all.

Oranna rode down the beach, passing only wreckage. Among the debris, she was able to find her weapons and satchel. However, she hadn't passed any bodies; not a single crew member was on this beach. This gave her an uneasy feeling as she turned her attention to the jungle. The sun was hanging low when Oranna dismounted amid some of the debris to construct a shelter and start a fire.

As the fire popped and crackled, Oranna gazed into its dancing flames, lost in thought when her concentration was shattered by the distant sound of drums. The rhythm was faint but growing steadily closer. Oranna swiftly dampened the fire and drew her urgrosh. The horse struggled against its tether, desperately trying to break free. Oranna cut the rope, and the horse bolted away. She stood at the ready, prepared to defend herself as the drumbeats grew louder. Now, the drums seemed to surround her, yet the darkness hid the source. Not even the stars offered their light in this pitch black night. The sound became deafening, and she spun around in the dark, feeling as though the shadows had hands reaching for her. But as abruptly as the drums started, they ceased. The only sounds that remained were the waves crashing onto the shore and her own breath quaking.

    Oranna remained alert for the rest of the night. When the sun finally rose, she embarked on a quest to find the source of the shadow drums. She carefully inspected her campsite for any traces of the drummers, but the beach appeared pristine, as if someone had erased all signs of their presence. Oranna knelt down and gathered a handful of sand. She raised it to her nose and inhaled. The scent of seawater and fish stung her nostrils. She exhaled and drew a deeper breath, detecting the lingering smell of horse and the remnants of her extinguished fire. On her third breath, her senses sharpened, and brow furrowed in concentration. This scent was intriguing, initially sweet but growing fouler as it lingered. Taking shorter breaths, she followed the intensifying fragrance.

The scent surrounded her campsite, leading her further down the beach. Oranna crouched low and followed it closely, her senses alert to her surroundings. The scent stretched far down the shore and into a small clearing within the jungle. She examined the opening among the trees and cautiously stepped into the dense, overgrown greenery.

Just a few feet into the thick jungle, she realized that all sounds had ceased. The waves' dancing, the wind whispering through the leaves, and even her own breath had vanished. Utter silence hung in the air. Bewildered, Oranna backed out of the jungle, and as her foot met the beach again, her ears were filled again with sound. Stepping back into the jungle, silence fell. She opened her mouth, but no sound emerged; she retreated onto the beach, and her voice rang out once more.

She sat on the beach and pondered what she had experienced. *"This must be some sort of cursed jungle,"* she thought, *"and if it is cursed then any survivors are in trouble."* She stood, weapon in hand, took a deep breath and ran into the jungle in search of her crew.

Within minutes of charging into the jungle, Oranna began to feel the weight of absolute silence around her. She slowed her run to a jog as she stayed on guard; without sound she needed to be vigilant. Scanning the trail and surroundings for any signs of life, but she saw nothing, yet she pressed forward.

Soon, she arrived at a small clearing. As she got closer, she realized she was on a cliff overlooking a waterfall. The water cascaded down into a sapphire pool below. Sunlight pierced through the mist of the falling water, refracting the light and sending rainbows dancing through the air. While she stood admiring nature, she had an eerie feeling of eyes burning through her. Slowly, she turned to see a large sabercat staring at her. It snarled as their eyes met. Oranna looked deep into its eyes and saw only hunger. Gripping her urgrosh tightly, she planted a foot, anticipating the strike.

She watched as the cat lowered its head, its muscles tensed, legs flexed and in a blink, it sailed towards her through the air. The cat's paws reached for her, its claws protruding. Oranna sidestepped and grazed the cat on the shoulder as it landed, spinning to face her again. She smiled while the sabercat snarled. They locked eyes once more, but something seemed different. The cat studied Oranna, as if calculating her movements. Oranna focused on the cat as its tail twitched.

Suddenly, the sabercat bolted to the side, leaping off a tree, and swiped its mighty paw at her. Caught off guard, Oranna barely rolled out of the way. The cat's claws grazed her left shoulder, drawing blood. Angry, Oranna rolled to her feet. She stepped forward, thrusting her urgrosh into its shoulder. The beast reared and thrashed in pain. Oranna stepped back, ready for another strike but found herself too close to the edge. She lost her balance on the loose rocks and slipped down the side of the cliff. The last thing she saw was the sabercat snarling down at her as she fell. Splashing into the water, its impact knocking her unconscious, she sank to the bottom of the sapphire pool.

  Oranna felt as if she was weightless, floating through the void. She knew not where she ended, and space began. She could feel nothing. *"Was this it? Was this death?"* she thought. She remembered the stories of the Elders, where, upon death, your soul becomes whole again and you are joined in the great hall with everyone that has lived. There, you feast, drink, and share tales of your deeds. You are finally free. At this moment, she didn't feel free. The air shifted, and Oranna heard a whisper in the wind. It was a familiar voice and made her smile. She reached for the amulet around her neck. The whisper was low, too low to hear. She searched the darkness for the source, but could not find it. The wind grew stronger, and the voice was louder, "AWAKE!" With a mighty jolt, Oranna sprang up. "Easy, calm down." Her eyes adjusted to the owner of the voice, and before her stood Maso.

"Where am I?" she said. "Currently in a hut, in a village in the jungle." Oranna sat up, stunned to see the captain alive. "How is this possible? I searched the beach, no one was there. I came into the jungle looking for you, and there was no sound and then a sabercat..."

"Hush now." the captain interrupted. "You had a hard fall and you need to rest. Lay back down, and I'll come back in a little while."

Oranna lay back down and fell asleep.

Oranna woke to the enticing smell of food and the joyful sound of laughter. She emerged from the hut to find a bustling village teeming with people. Fires roaring, and beasts roasted over them. Several children ran up to her. She took a step back but smiled as the children grabbed her hands and led her to a seat next to Captain Maso.

"Good to have you back," he laughed, handing her a plate. "What is all this?" she said.

"This is the village of Gleyma at the heart of the isle," he replied. "I thought this island was uncharted. And where are my injuries? How are so many of our crew still alive?"

Before the Captain could explain, the sound of a drum echoed through the air. Oranna's head ached as the memory of the shadow drums flashed in her mind. The entire village rose to its feet and started chanting. Oranna watched in confusion. "What is going on?"

"Quite he is coming," Maso said. "Who is coming?"

"The Lord." he replied and pointed.

Following his outstretched finger, Oranna could see an elven man being carried on a platform through the crowd. He stood about seven feet tall, wearing a golden cloak around his shoulders and a crown made of feathers and animal bones in his hair. As he moved through the crowd, the villagers bowed before him, and he threw fruits and flowers as he passed by. With a flick of his wrist, the platform stopped, and he descended.

Walking towards Oranna with his arms open, he greeted her saying, "Welcome to my village, my child. I am Lord Nasi. Please make yourself comfortable. Anything you need, I will provide for you, as I provide for all my children. Now let us celebrate life!" with a clap of his hands, he was back on the platform. Cheers rang through the crowd, and music filled the air as everyone began eating and dancing about the village.

"Isn't he wonderful?" said Maso. Oranna looked at him, a hint of unease in her eyes, "No, there is clearly something not right about him." Maso shot her a teasing look, "Someone sounds jealous!" he laughed. "Come, Oranna, have fun."

The night's celebration continued, and Oranna's suspicions grew. As she wandered the village, she stumbled upon most of the crew. While she was delighted to see them, she couldn't help but notice that none of them had any injuries. Even her own wounds seemed to have miraculously healed overnight. Feeling the need for some space, she made her way toward the river when a loud cheer erupted.

Oranna followed the sound and discovered a large crowd gathered around a pin. Curious, she asked a villager, "What is going on?"

"It is a fight between man and beast." the villager replied.

Oranna pushed her way through the crowd, her eyes widening, and her mouth falling open in shock. In the pin, she saw the sabercat she had battled on the cliffside. However, what was more shocking was who the sabercat was fighting. Her head began to spin, her limbs went numb, and she felt a sinking sensation in her stomach. The person fighting the sabercat was Jamison.

Jamison forcefully threw the sabercat against the rails and clutched its neck like a python. The beast struggled wildly, its claws scraping against the pin. Oranna watched in shock and horror. The sabercat's eyes met hers, this time she saw fear. She stood frozen, her gaze shifting to see Jamison, who stared at her with unblinking eyes. In a swift motion, he twisted the sabercat's neck, and the beast slumped over. The crowd erupted into cheers.

Pushing through the crowd to catch her breath, she was stopped by Maso."What's wrong?" he asked.

"He was dead, I saw him smash against the rocks."

"You are mistaken," Maso replied, his tone calm. "I told you Jamison was one of the strongest sailors I know."

Oranna pushed Maso back, her disbelief turning into frustration. "What happened to you?"

Maso reached for her, but Oranna reacted quickly. She grabbed his hand and threw him to the ground. With great haste she sprinted back to her hut, bursting through the door. She gathered her things, and made a dash for the jungle.

She could hear the shadow drums, like the previous night, surrounding her, blocking her from leaving the village. With every turn, there were more drums and villagers diverting her path. Determined, she continued to run towards the waterfall, intent on climbing her way out. Upon reaching the cliff, she began to climb, but her grip slipped, causing her to tumble back down. When she turned around, a chilling sight awaited her, the entire village now stood behind her. She stared at them, their eyes devoid of life, with only the flickering of torches casting eerie reflections off their blackened eyes.

The crowd parted, making way for Lord Nasi as he walked through. "Stay away from me!" Oranna shouted, her voice filled with defiance. Lord Nasi took a step forward, undeterred.

Oranna reached down and hurled a knife toward him. In a swift motion, he caught the blade with a casual swipe of his hand. Oranna's eyes widened in astonishment, and her hand instinctively searched for another weapon, but there was nothing. She clenched her fists, readying herself for a fight. "Please, my child come with me," Lord Nasi implored, taking a step closer. "Let me show you my work." Oranna scanned the crowd for a way out, but all exits were blocked.

Lord Nasi continued to approach, his tone softening. "Please, hear what I have to say, see what I have to show you. If you don't like it, you can leave. You have my word." He extended a hand toward her. With a deep scowl, Oranna reluctantly nodded, "Fine."
Lord Nasi smiled and raised his hand. Captain Maso hurried over and traced a symbol into the cliff. The rock face rumbled and shook, revealing an opening. "Follow me, my child." Lord Nasi beckoned, and he stepped through the opening. As Oranna entered, she glanced over her shoulder, watching as the crowd faded into the shadows.

Oranna found herself in a narrow stairwell that descended into darkness. Up ahead, she could see the soft glow of Lord Nasi's torch. She carefully made her way down the stone steps until she caught up to Lord Nasi.

"Why have we stopped?" She asked, her curiosity piqued.

"I didn't want you to miss it," Lord Nasi replied. He dipped the torch into a large brass basin at the bottom of the steps. With a whoosh, the basin burst into flames. The fire swiftly traveled through channels of oil, crisscrossing the chamber. Soon, the darkness was banished as the room was bathed in a warm, faint orange glow.

The chamber was expansive, adorned with intricate stone carvings. Tables and tools lay scattered around, and shelves displayed jars filled with peculiar creatures. High above them hung a curious orb emitting a bright green light. Oranna moved about cautiously, her curiosity mixed with unease. "What is this place?"

Lord Nasi, with a cryptic smile, replied, "This is my solitude, my castle, my haven." He strolled towards a table marred by the stains of dried blood. Orann's voice grew stern, "How did you come to this place, and what have you done to my friends?"

Lord Nasi regarded Oranna, his grin revealing rotten teeth, "I was once a healer for an Emperor, using herbs, potions, and my skills to mend wounds and alleviate pain. However, one day, while returning from a campaign across the sea, the Emperor's son fell ill. I tried everything at my disposal, but alas, death proved stronger. In her grief, the Queen Mother accused me of negligence, she convinced the Emperor, I had let the boy die. No matter how I pleaded, the Emperor could not be swayed. In his wisdom, he offered me a choice: death or life. I chose life, but the price was steep. I was marooned on this island, left to die a slow death. I begged the gods to take me, but they remained silent."

He continued his tale, his gaze distant. "I wandered the island for weeks, until one day,

I stumbled upon this cave. Here I studied the ancient carvings and discovered that these stones contained the spells for immortality. I managed to save my own life but soon found life without company was tedious. So, I began to retrieve bodies from wrecked ships and brought them back to serve a purpose. Some attempted to escape, not comprehending the vision of peace I had crafted. Using the stones, I created the Orb. Its green glow envelops the village, allowing us to live in peace. But if anyone ventures beyond its boundaries for too long, their bodies wither and fade to dust."

"So you keep them here as prisoners to do your will?"

"No, my child, they stay cause they want to live, and the world they left, that I left, is cruel and filled with people that don't understand greatness"

"What about me? Am I one of those things?"

"Unfortunately, you are not. You came to us alive, and my power only works on those that are at death's door." Lord Nasi picked up a small knife and held it in his boney hands. "You are very... strong."

Lord Nasi drew a heavy sigh, "Oranna, my child, give into my will. Live here forever." He took a step towards her.

Oranna stepped back and bumped into a shelf. A few jars containing creatures fell and shattered on the ground.

"I see beyond the veil, my child. I can bring him here." Oranna looked at him. "If you give me his amulet around your neck, I'll bring him back, and you two can live in happiness forever." Lord Nasi reached his hand out.

For a moment, Oranna thought it over. She could have him back in her life, they could be together, but at what cost? She looked into his eyes, "Never!"

"YOU ARE A FOOL, ORANNA OF THE NORTH. And for that, you must DIE."

Lord Nasi lunged at Oranna. She rolled to the right, and Lord Nasi knocked over the shelf. Glass shattered across the floor. Oranna picked up a large shard and stood to her feet.

"What are you going to do with that?" Lord Nasi laughed. "I can't die."

"Yes, you can." Oranna's eyes lifted to gaze at the orb. She threw the shard. "NOOO!" cried Lord Nasi as he rushed at her. Before he reached her, the shard shattered the orb, and green glass rained down.

Lord Nasi stepped forward, and Oranna watched as his skin began to shrivel, shatter, and shrink. His hand stretching out slowly turned to dust, and he fell to the floor. Looking up at her, he gargled and tried to form words. Oranna took her heel and drove it through his skull.

A loud crash startled her, and she turned to see that not only had Lord Nasi turned to dust, but the entire structure was withering as well. Oranna dashed for the stairs, her heart pounding. However, before she could reach them, the chamber began to cave in around her. She leaped back, panic rising, and spotted an opening in the ceiling. With the will to live fueling her strength, she scaled the rubble to reach the top. As the warm sunlight kissed her face, she saw the village, now decaying in disarray. The Villagers were disintegrating into dust, and the men in her crew were succumbing to the injuries they had sustained earlier. Her shoulder throbbing in pain and her wounds began to reopen.

Without hesitation, she sprinted for the path by the waterfall and saw Captain Maso standing in her way. "Oranna I'm sorry the voyage didn't turn out as planned."

"It's fine, come on, hurry, we can make it out of here." She grabbed his arm, and her fingers slipped away wet with blood.

"It's too late for me, but you can still leave. On the far side of the island, there is a cove with a few ships that were salvaged over the years. Some still float. Go, and you can make it."

She hesitated for a moment, her voice filled with urgency. "Captain, you don't have to stay. We can find a way to save you."

Maso managed a weak smile. "I've seen enough, Oranna. I've lived my fill. Now go, while you still have time."

Oranna peered at Captain Maso, determination in her eyes, as she heard the command in his voice. Honoring him, she simply said, "Yes, Captain."

As the barrier slowly faded, the island began to crack apart with a mighty earthquake. Oranna ran through the jungle as fast as she could, dodging the dying vegetation all around her. She made it to the beach and saw an old friend. She mounted the horse and headed for the cove. As she rode down the beach, she came upon a collection of ships and boarded the sturdiest of them. She pulled the sail, and it filled with wind, pushing her out of the cove and into open water. She looked back to see the island slowly sinking into the depths. As the last mountain slowly sank beneath the waves, Oranna smiled and laughed, knowing she would never forget the voyage to the Isle of the Forgotten.

The Fool King

Once there was a king in north
He was a fool at heart
His rule he declared henceforth
But he wasn't very smart

He rode around take what he will
Not caring who he hurt
He built his home on a hill
He thought it would keep him alert

He failed to be kind
And respect the serpent
He lost and went blind
Now he is a lonely servant

He wishes to be king again
But no subjects can he apprehend

From "*A Journey Home*" written by

The Bard

The Trials of King Horvath

"Whoa!" exclaimed the coachman, tugging on the reins to bring the wagon to a halt. The air felt thin and crisp, and Oranna could sense a mountain breeze brushing against her arms. Inhaling deeply, she caught the fragrant scent of cedar and moss hanging in the air. Although the hood obscured most of her view, she knew she was in the Ancestral Forest, nestled in the foothills of the Great Mountains.

The cage door screeched open, and rough hands dragged her out. She found herself thrust into a line alongside two others, their heads concealed beneath hoods, much like her own. It was apparent that the one in front of her was a Catfolk, the spotted tail swaying back and forth. Behind her stood a towering figure, emitting an unmistakable stench that she concluded was a Half-Giant.

    The guards guided them up a set of wooden steps and into a large hall. As the door swung open, a rush of warmth from the fire rushed over them. The hall was filled with a large gathering of people, yet an eerie silence hung in the air. The three prisoners were pushed past the central fire pit where a large elk was roasting. At the front of the hall, the guards forced them to their knees.

    Oranna's hood was swiftly removed, and her eyes took a moment to adjust to the room. It was a vast wooden hall adorned with ornate gold gilding. Her gaze was drawn to the front, where a frightening throne of bones stood, crafted primarily from animal bones. The throne loomed five feet above the others, its crown formed by two massive elk antlers and its armrests made of skulls. In the dim light, she could make out hands resting on them.

The hands braced themselves on the throne, and a shadowy figure emerged. Stepping into the light, it took Oranna an instant to recognize the imposing figure. He stood a monstrous seven feet tall, with shaggy gray hair cascading down to his shoulders and an even longer beard adorned with braids and trinkets of past glories, stretching down to his belly. A prominent scar marred his left eye. This towering presence could be none other than the self-proclaimed King of Barbarians, King Horvath.

King Horvath, who preferred to be known as "The Caring," was a determined and ferocious leader. Several years prior, he started raiding small villages in the Great Mountains, seizing whatever he desired and proclaiming himself as the King and Unifier of all the tribes. Those who refused to kneel were met with flames, while those who submitted, now pay him tribute. His followers mainly comprised mostly those that sought to save themselves from the fiery fate, although there are some that remain genuinely loyal to his banner.

"My glorious children, I have a treat for you. My Bear Guard scoured the kingdom for those who've escaped the King's justice, and they've delivered." he declared, with a cheer from the hall. "Before you, three of the most dangerous individuals to set foot in my kingdom. But fear not, for they shall receive true justice." The crowd erupted with excitement.

"First, we have this beautiful kitty cat from the southern swamps, Rantak. He stole a significant sum of gold from me, and we shall get it back… from his hide." King Horvath announced, placing a hand on Rantak's head. Rantak growled and snarled as King Horvath stepped back.

Smiling a wry smile at the close call, King Horvath shifted to the side. "Now, over here we have one almost as big as I am," the crowd laughed, while Oranna rolled her eyes. "Meet Barun, the Half-Giant!"

Barun stared into Horvath's eyes and began to rise, his powerful arms flexing, causing the ropes that bound him to twist and snap. Before he could take a step, the Bear Guard swiftly secured chains around his neck, dragging him down with a thunderous crash. "Ready to fight now, aren't we?" King Horvath quipped.

As King Horvath stepped forward to introduce Oranna, she seized the opportunity to act. Swiftly, she rolled back to free her hands, then sprang up and charged at Horvath. He swung a fist at her, but she ducked and kicked his legs out from under him, causing gasps from the onlookers.

As Horvath fell, Oranna turned to make her escape, but the Bear guard blocked her path. One guard approached from her left, but Rantak used his tail to trip him. With this distraction, Oranna tried to leap from the stage, but Horvath caught her ankle. He flung her into the edge of the firepit. Regaining his composure, he strode over to her, brushing the hair from his eyes, and catching his breath.

"Some of you might recognize this wretched woman," King Horvath declared, stooping to wrap his hand around Oranna's neck, lifting her for all to see. "She committed the gravest crime of all." His grip tightened. "She broke my heart, long ago, when we were betrothed. Now, my once future queen must face justice."

With a stern expression, he released her and returned to his throne. "Over the next three days, they will undergo a series of trials. If they complete them all, they will earn their freedom. But should they fail..." A sinister smile crossed his face. "DEATH!" The crowd erupted with a deafening cheer. "Take them away."

The Bear Guards collected the three captives, sending them off to the dungeon to await the Trials of King Horvath. The forest was silent as the final light faded into night. Oranna and her newfound companions sat in their cells, quietly contemplating their circumstances. Barun rubbed his neck where the chains had been, Rantak fidgeted with the lock, and Oranna stared into the night from the window.

"How much gold did you steal?" Barun grumbled, breaking the silence. "Not enough to deserve death," Rantak replied, continuing to work on the lock.

"What about you?" A sly grin appeared on Barun's face, "I bested him in a fight. He tried to convince my village that he was our king, so I challenged him, and beat him so badly he fled with his tail between his legs." Rantak burst into laughter.

Barun turned to Oranna. "And were you truly betrothed to that fool?" Without taking her eyes off the night, she nodded. Barun scoffed in disbelief. "Well, come on, tell the story." he coaxed.

With a deep sigh, Oranna turned to face her companions. "A long time ago, when Horvath was just beginning his raids, he arrived at my village. He threatened to burn and kill everyone unless they handed over the most beautiful woman. The elders decided that I should be the one, as I was of age and untainted. Horvath took me, and he burned the village anyway. We traveled for days to his fortress, and along the way, he killed and presented their deaths to me as gifts. On the seventh night, he brought me to his tent. He had been drinking heavily, and made advances, but I avoided his touch. I grabbed a rock and threw it as hard as I could, striking him just above the left eye, knocking him out. I slipped out as the guards slept, stole a horse, and rode high into the mountains until I found a quiet village that took me in."

Barun and Rantak sat in the cell, eyes wide and mouths agape, as Oranna chuckled and turned to the window. "If I know Horvath, he has something cruel planned for us tomorrow. We'd best get some rest." With that, the two settled down for the night, but Oranna couldn't sleep. She gazed into the sky, wondering if this might be the end.

The next morning, the companions awoke to the crowing of a rooster heralding the rising sun. Hooded and led from their cell, they walked through a fog shrouded forest, the only sound being the crunch of leaves underfoot. After some time, they came to an abrupt halt, and their hoods were ripped off. King Horvath stood before them, with a sizable crowd on either side.

"Good morn to each of you. I hope you rested well, for today you'll need your strength." Turning, King Horvath addressed the crowds, "As many of you know, I'm a selfless and humble person. I don't demand gold or trinkets. I have a deep love of all living things, which is why I collect exotic animals and creatures of distant lands." He paced back and forth. "For the first trial, I've released one of my favorite creatures into the woods, and one of you three must find it and bring it back to me."

He placed his hand over his heart. "This creature is immensely powerful and ferocious. Even while removing its chains this morning, it killed two of my men," which sent a shiver through the crowd. "The creature I'm speaking of is my wonderfully terrifying Ogre." A wicked smile peeled across his face.

He motioned to his guards, and they unchained the three. "Go on, move," one of the guards growled as he prodded Oranna with his spear. She looked at Horvath, "What are we to capture him with? Sticks and stones?" she asked.

"You'll have to figure that out," he replied. "Now, Run!" his voice boomed, and the three set off into the woods in search of the Ogre.

The three ran until they were well out of sight of the crowd, then slowed to a walk. "We should just keep running and never look back," Rantak suggested.

"I agree," Barun added. "If we keep running, by midday, we'll have covered so much ground they'll never catch us."

Both looked satisfied with this plan, but Oranna crossed her arms and asked, "How do you expect to outrun them?" She pointed to a nearby ridge, and Barun squinted while Rantak sniffed the air. Two Bear Guard men stood on the ridge. As they looked on, an arrow whizzed past Barun, and he stumbled back against a tree as it narrowly missed his face.

"They're watching us, like a hawk watches its prey," Oranna remarked. "So how far do you think you can go?" Barun shot her a disgusted look, let out a heavy sigh, and they continued their search.

By midday, the threesome had grown weary and rested under the shade of the Ancestral cedars. A refreshing breeze rustled through the trees, providing relief from their sweat drenched clothes.

"We've been running all day, and still no trace of this Ogre." Rantak grumbled. "Could it be a trick, and he never released the monster?"

Oranna shook her head. "He is not one for silly tricks." Rantak and Barun shrugged as they rested.

"You hear that?" Oranna stood, and the others listened.

"Water!" shouted Rantak. They jumped to their feet and rushed towards the sound of flowing water.

They reached a small waterfall that cascaded into a small pool and swam its way down through the forest. Rantak and Barun wasted no time, plunging their heads into the water and gulping down the sweet water. Oranna, more cautious, cupped her hands and slowly brought the water to her lips, while scanning the shore.

As the others complained about the heat, a shadow suddenly passed over the sun. "Quit your heavy breathing, Barun." hissed Rantak. "I'm breathing normally; you're the one making that gurgling sound." An angry look crossed Rantak's face. "I would never gurgle, you overgrown tree."

"OVERGROWN TREE!" Barun's face reddened, and they rushed each other, ready to fight. Oranna stood between them, her hands outstretched in a plea for peace.

They looked at her in bewilderment, her gaze was fixed towards the top of the waterfall. They turned to see what had captured her attention. What they initially thought was a cloud blocking the sun had a suspicious large shape -more like a monster. They squinted to see through the light, and the shadow emitted a blood curdling growl before leaping from the waterfall and crashing into the pool below.

The Ogre had found them.

The Ogre thrashed in the water, sending waves splashing over the threesome, who stared in silence, awaiting an attack. Barun and Rantak exchanged a quick nod before rushing into the waves. The Orge, startled, turned to face them, and emerged from the water. It stood, from toe to head it was about nine feet tall, with a greenish gray hue, red eyes, and a menacing snarl that revealed sharp tusks and rows of pointed teeth. Its arms were as large as Rantak.

It splashed them and snorted, Barun grabbed a large rock from the water and hurled it at the creature. The rock struck the Ogre squarely between the eyes, knocking it back. It turned, blood running down its face, and wailed. It glared at Barun and in a flash the Ogre was on top of him. Barun, who fought for his life, landed punches that did little damage. The Ogre seized Barun's hand and squeezed, prompting a desperate plea, "Get this thing off me!"

The Ogre leaned down and, with one swift jerk of his head, bit off Barun's right hand.

As the Ogre went in for a second bite, Rantak leaped onto its back. The Ogre turned and stomped, trying everything to remove him. It reached back with its long arms and seized Rantak's tail, causing him to scream as the Ogre hurled him into some rocks.

The Ogre charged through the water, snarling and growling, swiping its hands through the water and flinging a fallen tree branch. It spun in the water, baring its teeth and splashing water around.

Oranna watched the creature's behavior and realized it was acting like a child throwing a tantrum. "Could this be a baby Ogre?" she thought. She Slowly waded into the water, and the Ogre turned and growled in response. Oranna extended her hand and began to make soothing sounds. The Ogre splashed and spun in a circle. Oranna inched closer, playfully splashing water back at the Ogre, which seemed to delight in it.

The Ogre laughed and splashed Oranna again, then moved through the water. Oranna splashed back, and the Ogre laughed louder this time. To the shock of the others, Oranna had managed to tame the Ogre through play. She reached up to caress its face, and the Ogre closed its eyes, leaning into her touch.

Rantak wrapped Barun's arm with moss and strips of cloth, while Oranna continued to engage the Ogre. "What are we supposed to do with a baby?" Barun complained. "We can't take it back to be a prisoner in his menagerie."

Rantak looked up from his work, "If we don't bring it back, they will kill us."

Barun shook his head and winced as the bandage was tied tightly. "Thoughts Oranna?"

She glanced over her shoulder at the others and then back at the Ogre. "We take it back and devise a plan to escape with our new friend."

Rantak and Barun exchanged looks and laughed. "You expect us to risk our lives to save that dim witted creator that took my hand?" Barun asked.

"I expect you to have the courage to stand when others can't," Oranna replied, and Barun blushed. "What is your plan then?"

Oranna turned and shrugged. "I am working on it. But we do need to get back, the sun is setting soon."

The two nodded and rose to their feet, collecting water as they prepared to make their return.

As the starlight filled the night, Horvath puffed on his pipe, and the glow of torches illuminated him. He turned to the small crowd. "Well it appears they've died, and I'm down an Ogre." he laughed, "Enough time wasting; a feast awaits us."

He and the crowd began to leave, but a shout stopped them. Everyone turned to see. Over the rise about a hundred yards away the four came strolling back. Horvath choked and coughed on his pipe. Barun and Rantak held hands with the Ogre, while Oranna rode on its shoulders. The crowd erupted in cheers and surged past Horvath to greet the triumphant group.

Horvath's temper flared, "CHAIN THEM IMMEDIATELY!" He ordered his men. Chains were thrown around the Ogre and the three before the crowd could get too close. The Ogre wailed and pulled on his chains. Oranna looked at the frightened Ogre, calming its spirits. The three were hooded and taken away.

Their hoods were removed as the guards pushed them back into their cells and locked the door. Barun growled as he gripped his wounded forearm. "Do you think they'll send for a healer?" he asked, with a slight quiver in his voice.

Oranna shook her head. "I suspect he hopes you'll be dead with infection by morning."

Rantak unwrapped the bandages, and a foul smell stung his nostrils. "Rot is setting in. What should we do?" he asked. Oranna was already moving into action. She reached out of the cell for a torch, but her reach fell short. Her nails scraped at the wooden handle, and a slow moving, fuzzy snake slithered towards it.

Rantak's tail extended, wrapping around the torch. "It's a useful tool," he said, smiling, as he recoiled his tail with the torch. Oranna took it over to Barun, who nodded in understanding. They pressed the flame against his wound, causing Barun to cry out and the smell of smoldering flesh filled the air. They wrapped the cleanest cloth around it, and Barun looked up to Oranna, "What's the plan of escape?"

A smile crossed Oranna's face.

At sunrise, the three were brought to the side of the rushing river. Horvath spoke, "This great river, which brings life to us all, will be the stage of today's endurance trial." His words spilled from his mouth with bitterness, like sour milk from a cat's dish. "The guests of honor shall be placed in cages above the water, each with the chain that suspends their cage. If they can endure and hold it till sundown, they live. But if they fail, they shall crash into the freezing water and die!" The crowd cheered, and the three were placed in their cages, each gripped their chains and the trail of endurance began.

Oranna faced the trial of endurance without fear, having once endured a suspension over a gorge in the mines of Gromdune for three days. She knew her strength would hold. She glanced at Rantak, recognizing his strength and agility, and for such a small stature, which rivaled the gods. He gripped the chain with his right hand and his tail, ready to switch when fatigue set in. She was confident he would survive this day.

Then, her gaze turned to Barun. Half-Giants were incredibly strong, but with only one hand, doubt washed over her. "Barun?" Worry tinged her voice.

"I will be fine," Barun reassured her, though his words brought little comfort.

As the sun rose high, all three still clung to their chains, but most of the crowd had grown bored and left in search of other entertainment. Horvath and a few guards remained, their cages having moved only slightly.

"You all bore me," Horvath muttered, spitting on the ground. "I seriously thought the gimp would have fallen by now!"

Barun turned to look and accidentally slipped his cage down. "Ah, now we're getting somewhere." He tightened his grip, and Horvath rolled his eyes.

"What of you, wench? Getting tired yet?" Horvath taunted Oranna. She stared back at him and Horvath scoffed, "That's all you can do is stare?" She responded with a boot flying past his head. The three in cages laughed, and a guard joined in.

Horvath turned, saying, "Haha, so funny, isn't it?" The guard straightened up, but Horvath continued, "No, please continue to laugh."

Horvath stood, and put his arm around the guard's shoulders and said, "I hope you laugh on your trip to Hel." and with a push, sent the guard into the frigid current. The other guard's looked soberly ahead. "Now *that* is funny." Returning to his seat, Horvath sat down, pleased with himself.

Under the scorching midday sun, Oranna's shoulders ached. Horvath had grown tired of the trial. Oranna asked, "Barun? Rantak? How are you holding up?"

"I am tired, but I will manage." Rantak replied with a smirk.

Barun, drenched in sweat and strained, said, "I've been better."

Oranna encouraged them, "Hold on. Just a few more hours, and maybe we can enact our plan."

"What Plan?" Horvath's voice barked. "I hope you aren't planning to escape because that nullifies our agreement."

"My only agreement is to kill you, Horvath," Oranna stated firmly, eliciting laughter from the others.

Horvath retorted, "So full of yourself. Have you forgot, you're in *my* cages? I'll decide your fate!"

Oranna challenged, "The only thing you'll decide is if you'll beg on your knees or your back."

Horvath stared unblinkingly at her, then he noticed Barun's worsening condition, "Looks like your friend isn't doing well."

Oranna turned to see Barun slipping further down his chain, his cage taking on water.

"Well, this won't do, you're probably hungry," Horvath said with a sneer. "How about some honey." Horvath nodded, and a guard dropped a beehive above their cages. The hive fell and landed on Barun's cage.

"Enjoy the honey. I'll see you at sundown." Horvath snapped his fingers, and he and his guards left. Bees swarmed and stung Barun, causing him to grunt and his right eye to swell shut.

Oranna began to rock her cage, causing it to swing. "Hold on, Barun," she urged.

Barun grunted as multiple bees stung his flesh, his face swelling beyond recognition. Oranna's cage swung over, and she tipped the beehive, but didn't knock it off. "Oranna, save your energy." Barun roared, as his cage sank lower into the water, with it now rushed over his knees.

"No, Barun, I can save you, just hold on." Oranna said as her cage came closer.

"It is fine, my end is here," Barun smiled and let go of his chain. His cage splashed into the water. Oranna was speechless, and Rantak let out a loud cry. They watched as the cage sank, and Barun disappeared beneath the churning water.

As the light faded from the forest, Oranna and Rantak continued to hold on. They heard clapping as Horvath approached. "What a shame that your friend couldn't hold on," Horvath remarked as their cages were lowered. "I guess he didn't like honey."

As his cage door opened, Rantak leaped out, claws drawn, and slashed at Horvath. The claws caught one of his braids. Horvath kicked the weakened Rantak to the ground, and the guards seized him. "Your doom will come tomorrow," Horvath said through gritted teeth.

"Your doom will come tomorrow at my hand." Oranna retorted.

Horvath glared at her and ordered, "Take them away."

Back in their cell they performed a small honoring ceremony for Barun. "What will we do now?" Asked Rantak. "Rest." Oranna said solemnly. "What of our plan? With Barun gone the plan has a large hole in it."

"We will think of something. Now try to rest." Oranna knew if she didn't plan for something, tomorrow would mean death.

Oranna rose as morning hung in the air. She looked around, but Rantak was nowhere to be seen. The door to the cell swung open, and three guards entered. "Get up," demanded one of the guards. Oranna stood, and they chained her hands, leading her down a long, dark hall. The sound of buzzing flies and the pungent smell of blood surrounded her. She could hear a crowd chanting, "Blood, Blood, Blood." and then the crowd erupted in cheers. The guards chained her to the wall. As she glanced around the room, she spotted a figure in the corner.

"Rantak!" she exclaimed with surprise in her voice. "I thought you were dead."

Rantak looked at her and stepped into the light, his body was covered in cuts and bruises. "I...have fought...three times," Rantak's speech was labored.

"Fought what?" Oranna asked.

"Everything from wild beasts to men," Rantak gasped, taking in a deep breath. "He will fight me to my death. I wished for my life to end in the land of my ancestors, but it looks like it will not." His ears twitched as a tear rolled down his cheek.

Before Oranna could respond, the large arena gates opened, and the guards dragged a corpse in. "Cat, your turn again." The guards seized Rantak, and he could barely put up a fight. Rantak looked back and said, "Oranna, kill these bastards for me." He managed a smile before being pushed into the light, and the gates slammed shut.

Oranna waited with bated breath. Beneath the arena, the room was dusty and oppressively hot, the air thick with the stench of death. Then she heard what she had feared. The roar of the crowd meant one thing: blood had been spilled. Oranna could feel the chains that bound her shaking as the crowd cheered. The gate to the arena swung open, flooding the room with light. Two guards dragged in Rantak's lifeless body and callously threw it onto the pile of that day's victims. She choked back tears as Rantak's lifeless body lay before her.

Oranna was the last one left to face the horrors of the arena. The guards approached her, carefully unlocked her chains and guided her up the ramp towards the gate. Light engulfed Oranna as she stepped into the arena. It was circular, with two gates – one leading to the pit where victims were held, and the other for storing the creatures. In the center of the arena stood five stone pillars surrounding a star-shaped floor. Flags bearing the crest of King Horvath adorned the battlements. A loud voice resounded, "Welcome our final challenger to confront the horrors graciously provided by the loving King Horvath, all the way from the North, we have Oranna!" The crowd responded with boos and hurled rotten food at her. Oranna quickly dodged the incoming projectiles.

"She moves quickly, she will need that as she faces the prized Golden Serpent!" The crowd erupted in cheers. Oranna scanned her surroundings but couldn't see anything. The sound of metal scraping rang through the arena and the gate across from her slowly creaked open. A shadow came slithering out of the darkness and coiled up in the light. Oranna now saw a thirty-foot serpent coiled before her, its golden scales adorned with black diamond shapes along its back. The creatures had jet-black eyes and a bright red tongue. It stared at her, unmoving. Oranna took a cautious step, and the serpent hissed. She noticed fangs the size of her arm filling its mouth, realizing that this wasn't a fight but a slaughter.

    The crowd erupted in cheers as the serpent and Oranna locked eyes. She took a deep breath, focusing on drowning out the noise of the crowd. Her eyes darted around, forming a plan. Today, she wouldn't meet her end; instead, she intended to keep her promise to kill Horvath. Scanning the arena, her gaze met Horvath's. He sat smugly in a large chair, wearing a toothy grin. He gave her a mocking little wave. Oranna spat on the ground and locked eyes with the serpent. To execute her plan, she needed to act swiftly.

    As she stepped forward, the serpent began to slither to her right. She shuffled to the left to keep the serpent in front of her. It moved faster, and she spun on her heel as the serpent flanked her. With its mouth agape,It charged at her, and she rolled to the left, narrowly evading its attack. The crowd groaned in disappointment.

She sprang to her feet just as the serpent's large fangs sank deep into the ground before her. With a quick kick to the nose, the serpent reared in anger and shook its head. Oranna seized the opportunity and dashed past it to reach the center of the arena. The crowd roared with excitement, and Horvath appeared pleased to see her on the run.

The serpent regained its sense and turned to locate Oranna. It lunged at her, but she skillfully ducked behind a pillar. The serpent moved around the pillars, hunting for her. Oranna stood her ground in the center of the star. The serpent reared up, looming above her, its eyes stared daggers into her. Its venom-dripping fangs poised to strike. Oranna took a step back, at the serpent's lunge, she sprang backward, vaulting over its scaly body. The serpent's fangs sank deep into its own flesh, and its eyes widened in agony.

Oranna smiled as she reached down and grabbed a rock. Leaping onto the serpent's neck, with the rock held high above her head, she locked eyes with Horvath and grinned. With all her strength, she brought the rock down, burying it deep within the serpent's skull.

The crowd fell into a hushed silence as they watched Oranna climb down from the slain serpent. She looked up, arms raised, and the crowd erupted in a deafening roar. Then, she turned her gaze toward Horvath. His eyes blazed with anger as he starred back. In a fury, he ripped off his royal cape and cast it into his chair, drawing his axe, and leapt into the arena.

"You die today, bitch," he snarled at her, his voice dripping with rage.

"You first," Oranna retorted, further fueling Horvath's madness. He let out a roar and charged at her, his axe raised high above his head. Despite his size, he moved surprisingly fast, and his axe came down, narrowly missing Oranna. She countered with a left fist to his eye, but it barely even shook him. He raised his axe once more and swung it fiercely, spittle flying through the air as he screamed.

    His axe moved so swiftly that Oranna's hair was blown back as she jumped and scrambled to evade each strike. She moved cautiously until her back pressed against a pillar. Horvath stopped in front of her, his anger growing with each missed strike. Between breaths, he declared, "You die," and raised his axe high for another blow.

    Oranna dropped to the ground and looked up. Horvath had stood too close, and now his ax was embedded in the pillar. She delivered a powerful punch to his gut, forcing the air flying out of him. She followed it with a kick to his right knee, producing an audible crack as he fell to his knees. He clutched his body, gasping for breath.

Oranna stood and reached out, snapping the handle of his axe. She tilted Horvath's head up and locked eyes with him. "I missed the first time, but I've gotten better," she declared. With that, she drove the broken handle into his left eye. Horvath, the self proclaimed King of the North, met his demise.

The crowd erupted in cheers and screams, beginning to stampede out of the arena. Oranna made her way toward the gate leading to the creatures' enclosure, but several of the Bear Guard blocked her path. With a clench of her fist, the men dropped their weapons and knelt before her. Oranna brushed past them and pushed open the large gate.

She started to free the animals and creatures that Horvath had held captive in his menagerie. As she opened the last gate, there sat the baby Ogre. It snarled at first, but then recognized Oranna. Its eyes softened, and it smiled as she unclasped his chains. The Ogre shuffled to the open gate and looked out, then back at Oranna. She nodded, and the Ogre took off at a full sprint, finally free.

Oranna gathered her belongings, saddled a horse, and carefully secured the body of Rantak. She said a warrior's prayer over his body and whispered, "I'll take you home, my friend." With a determined heart, she mounted her horse and set off on her journey south. Following her were a few of the Bear Guard who had sworn their allegiance to her. A smile graced her lips as the once King of the North's fortress lit up the night.

The Colossal Beast

Legend tells of the colossal beast
That's shadow haunts the far East
Wings of fire and tail of thorns
They say it has black metal horns

Undaunted by mortal tastes
Human souls it lays to waste
Lion head with fangs so sharp
It was defeated with golden harp

1000 years it will sleep
So they built a giant keep
6000 guard the monstrous walls
While it sleeps cozy within its halls

Every move it does make
They pray it will not wake
One day soon it's slumber will end
And all those guards must defend

For snacks of souls it will want to feast
So says the legend of the Colossal Beast

From "*A Journey Home*" written by
The Bard

Fight on Black Sands

On the northwestern coast of Edoria, a mysterious beach exists. The legend has it that the elven warrior, Gannondor, had acquired the Flame Sword, a blade forged with the sole purpose of destroying Giants. With this sword, Gannondor the Bold and his soldiers drove a horde of monsters led by Zola of the Mountain Giants, to the Western sea. On the sandy shores, Gannondor thrust his blade deep into Zola's heart. The Giant's body cracked and shuddered. He began to glow and burst into millions of pieces. When the smoke had dissipated, Zola was defeated. Both the Flame Sword and its wielder, Gannondor, had vanished, leaving the beach scorched black. To this day, it is known as the Black Sands of Zola.

The Bard concluded his song with a melancholic strum and bowed his head. The men in the tavern clapped, and the women swooned, tossing coins into his hat. Collecting his tips, The Bard retreated to the back of the tavern. His eyes brimmed with glee as he beheld the cooked chicken and frothy mead laid before him. Just as he was about to sink his teeth into the first bite, a voice from behind interrupted him.

"Tell me, are your songs your tales or are the deeds of others?" The Bard slowly turned, meeting the eyes of Oranna of the North. Fear soaked The Bard, a tremble quivered in his throat as Oranna's eyes pierced him with a ferocity akin to a storm on the Mist sea. Suddenly, she flickered, and The Bard screamed, dropping his chicken. A smile spread across her face, and The Bard clutched his chest. "Don't frighten me like that." Laughter bubbled forth as two embraced, reuniting like old friends.

For the better part of the evening, Oranna and The Bard lingered in the Lakemoon Tavern, savoring drinks, sharing tales of their adventures, and reminiscing about their times together. As the night ebbed away, Oranna took a hearty gulp from her drink, slamming it onto the table. The Bard chuckled, but Oranna swiftly hushed him. "I have a question for you," she said through slowed lips. The Bard, now looking a bit drowsy, nodded in response.

"Since I was young, you've sung songs of the Black Sands of Zola. True?" Again, the Bard nodded.

"Tell me then..." She hiccupped, "Is it a real place or figment of imagination?"

The Bard's face turned from drowsy to serious. He straightened up, clearing his throat. "It's real," he declared. Oranna's eyes sparkled with wonder. "Have you been there?"

The Bard shook his head. "Alas, my dear, I wander from town to town. I do not dare venture into the wilds." He took a swig from his cup.

Oranna regarded him for a moment and replied, "Do you know the way?"

The Bard stopped drinking and set his cup down. He stared at her. "If you head west until you reach the Tail of the Taran, there you will find a hidden pass that will take you on the mountain's edge. You will reach the end of the road and head down into the clouds and across the emerald sea. And if you make it there alive, your eyes will see the Black Sands." He picked up his cup and resumed drinking.

Oranna pondered what she had just been told. In an instant, she stood. "That settles it. We are going to see the Black Sands of Zola!" But after hours of drinking and standing up abruptly, she passed out and fell like a sleeping giant on the table. The next morning, Oranna and The Bard gathered up some supplies and set out west to the Taran Mountains.

The Bard and Oranna embarked on the main road. The morning sun shimmered and danced on the glassy lakes, while the breeze swayed the trees, rustling the leaves. Birds chirped in their nests, while others were gracefully gliding through the blue sky. Insects darted and buzzed around the wildflowers blooming in the meadows and grasses that enveloped the Land of Lakes. As the morning became afternoon, the two companions found rest under a large oak.

"We should get moving. We still have a few more hours of good daylight, and there aren't many villages left on the main road," Oranna said as she rose, swinging her pack over her shoulder. The Bard remained lying on the ground, his hat covering his face, unmoved by her words. Oranna tapped him with her foot. "Did your ears hear me?" The Bard responded by snoring louder. Oranna stared down at him. "Are we going to have to do this the easy way or the hard way?" Once again, The Bard snored and rolled on his side.

She sighed. "I guess the hard way." With resolve, she walked to the main road, stooping to picking up a few rocks. With precision, she threw the first pebble near his arm, then the next bounced off his hat. A chuckle emerged from under the hat. "You'll have to do better than that," came the muffled voice.

Oranna narrowed her eyes, and a gust of wind followed as The Bard sat up, turning to see a rock embedded in a nearby tree and a hole in his hat's brim. He looked back at Oranna, who smiled, casually tossing another rock in her hand. Without delay, The Bard bounced to his feet. "I think it is time to go. Don't just stand there." he said, hastening down the road.

As the sun dipped below the horizon, the silhouette of the Tail of Taran could be seen in the distance. Oranna and The Bard arrived at Nadir's Reach, the last village on the main road leading west from the Land of Lakes. The tavern, though dreary, boasted the renowned Norden Mead. The Bard livened up the place with a few melodious songs, which earned both him and Oranna a complimentary meal. Exhausted, the two crawled into their beds, but slept an uncomfortable sleep.

    At the break of dawn, the rooster's crow stirred them from slumber, Oranna and the Bard rose to gather their belongings. They made their way to the northwestern edge of the village, embarking upon an old hunting trail. "Are you certain you want to do this?" The Bard's words soaked with concern. "Yes," Oranna affirmed, she stepped on the trail and forged ahead. The Bard shrugged and followed suit.

    Morning arrived swiftly as they continued along the trail, which had become horribly overgrown, strewn with thorns and obstructed by fallen trees. Insects buzzed incessantly around their heads as they pressed on. Thick branches overhead choked out the sunlight, casting shadows along the path. The morning heat intensified rapidly, as beads of sweat trickled down their faces.

    By midday, the two were very tired and stopped at a small stream. The Bard plopped down with a grunt, "How much further? It feels like we've been walking for days." Oranna smiled and drank from her waterskin as The Bard continued to complain. She sat through his whining and focused on her breathing. She closed her eyes; she could smell the dirt and water as the stream trickled on. She felt the slight breeze as it moved through the trees and kissed her skin. She heard the slow songs of the birds and then she heard something else. She placed her hand over the Bard's mouth, "Shh." She surveyed her surroundings.

    "What is it?" The Bard scrambled behind her. "Are we in danger?" Slowly Oranna drew her knife. She held it up close to her face, surveying the area for the intruder. She took a deep breath and sliced through the air as her blade turned end over end and struck a tree.

A fingertip's width below her blade was the target. The Bard gasped, and Oranna's eyes grew soft. There, beneath the blade's edge, was a child. The female child stood still, eyes closed, holding her breath. She had shoulder-length red hair, round cheeks, and a thin nose. Standing around four feet tall, she wore dirt-covered clothes, an old leather belt with a small pouch, and a carving knife attached to it. Slowly, she opened one eye and looked at the two.

"Am I dead?" Oranna and The Bard shook their heads. "Oh, good." She opened both eyes and cheerfully stepped out from under the knife. "Hello, my name is Ellka." Before Oranna or the Bard could reply, she continued, "You don't have to tell me your names; I know you are The Bard, the world's greatest singer and songwriter. You have traveled a thousand roads and loved even more, but you have gotten kind of fat." The Bard's smile of pride was quickly shattered. "And you are the strong warrior of the north that has battled armies and sailed the seas. You are Oranna." Oranna smiled and nodded.

Ellka looked at them both. "Are you two married?" The companions started to stutter and stumble over their words, talking over each other in confusion. Oranna took a deep breath and turned towards Ellka. "Ellka, what are you doing out here?"

Ellka smiled, "I saw you perform last night in Nadir's Reach, and I overheard you talking about going to see the Black Sands, and I wanted to come. So, I gathered my things." She opens her pouch, pulling out a slice of bread, hard cheese, and a few gold coins. "Then I followed you into the forest."

Oranna looked at her, "What about your family? Won't they be worried about you."

Ellka's cheerful demeanor faded. "I don't have a mama or papa."

The Bard interjected, "That's nonsense; everyone has parents." Oranna glared at The Bard.

"My papa was killed during the raid on Orasul, and my mama went into the woods to gather food for us and never came back."

Oranna stood and pulled on The Bard's arm, "We can't leave this child out here." The Bard appeared shocked, "We can't take this child with us."

"She has no one else," Oranna said, locking eyes with him. The Bard glanced between Oranna and Ellka.

"Fine, but you are responsible if she is eaten by a lion." Oranna playfully hit his arm and turned to Ellka.

"You can come with us to the Black Sands. But you must do what we say and listen when we say it." Ellka's excitement couldn't be contained as she began to jump up and down.

"You won't have to worry about me. Let me help with your things." She rushed over and grabbed Oranna's pack, attempting to lift it. Oranna smiled and gently took it from Ellka's willing hands.

"I can manage, but thanks for the help." Ellka grinned, and the three fell in line, resuming their walk together down the path.

The threesome ventured into the late afternoon. The scorching sun was concealed by large, dark clouds that filled the sky. The very air around them seemed to turn a greenish hue. Trees began to crash around them as the winds intensified. Thunder rumbled, and lightning sparked the sky. The temperature plummeted, prompting Oranna to wrap a cloak around herself to ward off the chill. The Bard buttoned his coat and turned his collar up. Oranna noticed Ellka shivering beneath her tattered clothes. She reached into her pack and retrieved a blanket, tearing off a small piece with her knife to wrap around Ellka.

The rain poured down, transforming the dirt path into thick mud. Their boots grew heavy with caked muke, each step more grueling than the last. As they went on, the dense forest thinned, revealing outcroppings of rock faces. Their journey became perilous as the relentless rain persisted. The once small dirt path they followed had become a mire of murky water and loose rocks, surging under their feet. Oranna halted and surveyed the path ahead. A section of missing earth blocked their way. "Are we stuck?" The Bard asked. Oranna remained silent, searching for a way to cross.

"Do we have rope?" Ellka inquired, attempting to open The Bard's pack. He removed his pack, pulling out coiled rope. "Give it here," Oranna said sternly. She quickly tied a loop and began swinging it. With skill, she landed the loop around a large rock about ten feet above them on the other side.

"Here," she handed it to The Bard. "Swing across." The Bard's face twisted with confusion.

"Gods no. Why me?" Oranna looked him up and down. "You're the largest of us. If it can hold you, it can hold any of us." The Bard appeared less confused but more agitated.

"And if I fall?" Oranna simply held the rope out to him.

The Bard rolled his eyes and sighed deeply. "At least you can't see that I am crying with all the rain." Stepping back, he took a deep breath. With a running leap, he swung out over the gap. The rope became taut, and The Bard swung safely to the other side. Surprised and cheerful, he glanced back at the others. With a grin, he tossed the rope back to Oranna and Ellka.

Oranna secured their packs to the rope and swung them over to The Bard. Once on the other side, it was Ellka's turn. She stepped to the gap cautiously. "I'm afraid," she said looking at the gap.

"Just look at him, and he will catch you," Oranna reassured, pointing towards the Bard, who awaited Ellka eagerly. She nodded, trembling slightly, and edged closer to the gap. With a deep breath, she jumped. With a loud scream, she swung across and landed right into The Bard's waiting arms. "See, not so scary," Oranna shouted. The two laughed and tossed the rope back to Oranna.

She gripped the rope tightly, giving it a firm tug before taking a step back and dashing off the edge. As she swung, lightning crackled down and struck the rock, causing the rope to snap, and she fell. Reacting swiftly, The Bard leaped out and caught Oranna's hand. Straining and grunting, he hoisted Oranna up the embankment. Ellka clung to The Bard's waist, assisting in pulling him back. Exhausted, the three slumped atop each other, drawing in heavy breaths. Oranna acknowledged The Bard with a nod, though he brushed it off casually. Ellka sat up with a grin, "That was fun. Let's do it again!" Both Oranna and The Bard groaned.

After picking themselves up and resting for a bit, they trudged on down the path. The clouds parted, and the sun's rays danced on the rain soaked landscape. The threesome crested a hill that overlooked the valley. Ellka stopped and marveled at the scenery. "This is so beautiful." Oranna and The Bard both paused, admiring the view as well. In the west, the Tail of the Taran's jagged peaks outlined the sky as the sun slowly sank behind them. The valley beneath lay bathed in shadow, the pinks and purples of the setting sun painted the trees. The beauty overtook them and as they gazed at the wondrous colors.

The silence was broken by Oranna, "We must make haste," she declared, pointing into the valley. Nestled in the foothills before them, faint wisps of smoke rose from chimneys. "If we hurry, maybe we can make supper." Oranna grinned. Excitement fueled them as they continued their journey, eager to reach the village.

The early evening air settled in around them, a thin silvery fog hovered over the valley. Following the wisps of smoke, they arrived at a small settlement. Passing through a rustic wooden gate along the path, a sign above them read 'Satul.' They passed several wooden structures resembling houses, each telling its own tale. One building boasted antlers adorning the doorframe, with pelts and hides draped over the railings. Next to it stood another structure enclosed by a small wooden fence, a garden brimming with sprouting flowers and wheat stocks.

The threesome traced the scent of smoke and followed the fires glow to the last house nestled within the settlement. Echoes of laughter and cheerful chatter could be heard through the wooden walls. Oranna touched the old handle, feeling its rough edges in her hand. With a push, the heavy door creaked open. They stepped through the door, into the warmth and comfort of a crackling fire. The structure was old, its timbered walls were weathered and cracked by time. The room was small, and filled with swirling smoke from the roaring fire. However, the chatter and laughter abruptly stopped. Oranna, The Bard and Ellka were met by every face in the room, staring at them with a cautious curiosity.

    The Bard unbuttoned his coat and shook off the rain, neatly folding it before placing it over a nearby chair. Taking a seat, he looked at each face staring at him. "I'd love some bread... and chicken... and whatever drink you have, preferably an ale." Blank stares greeted his request. He glanced at Oranna and Ellka, shrugging in puzzlement. A very elderly woman scooted her chair out and shuffled over to a counter. She pulled out a plate and utensils, she placed a cold chicken breast and a hunk of bread upon it. Pouring a pint of ale, it frothed over the brim and dribbled down the sides. She carried the offerings to The Bard, and placed it down before him. "Thank you," he said, seizing the pint and gulping it down, before taking a huge bite of the bread. Looking up at everyone still staring, he belched. "This is very good. Can my friends have some too?" The elderly woman looked Oranna and Ellka up and down, nodding slightly. As she did, many in the room turned back and began chattering and carrying on, as if they had never entered.

Oranna sank into her seat with a sigh while Ellka pulled her chair closer. "You are very rude," Ellka said sharply.

The Bard burped, "How so?" he mumbled through a mouth of chicken.

"We are strangers here, and you barge in as if it's some tavern you've played in." Oranna whispered, her voice tight with concern. "This settlement isn't on the map. We need to be cautious." As the words left her lips, two plates slid onto the table. Oranna glanced up, greeted by the toothless grin of the elderly woman who then shuffled back to her seat. Oranna remained watchful. "I don't know if I trust them," she confessed, turning back to find both Ellka and The Bard digging into the chicken like wild dogs. Oranna sat back in her chair, keeping a watchful eye on the room as the others resumed their conversations.

Their bellies full, each sat back and started to relax. The warmth from the crackling fire felt like a fur blanket wrapped about them. Shadows danced on the walls, as the glow of the fire illuminated the weathered timbers of the place. The Bard and Oranna regaled Ellka with jokes and tales. The Bard embellished and over exaggerated, in his usual style, captivating the attention of a few settlers who turned to listen. He spun tales of woe and strife, and far off shores. Gradually, the entire room was eagerly listening to The Bard's tales, hanging on every word. During his third story, a tall man with shaggy gray hair and a stubbled beard slid beside Oranna. She briefly glanced at him before turning back to listen. The man's pungent odor of garlic and onions wafted into

Oranna's nose and made her gag. With blackened teeth, the man grinned, "How are you?" His voice was soaked with charm and ale.

"Name's Galen. What is a pretty thing like you doing here?" Oranna paid no mind to his questions and sat watching the Bard. Irritated by her disregard, Galen cleared his throat, demanding, "I asked for your name, woman." He stood and puffed out his chest, but Oranna continued to ignore him. Growing increasingly frustrated, Galen let out a sigh of anger and grabbed her chair, "When I talk, you answer…" as he twirled her around he was met with a glint of steel as Oranna swiftly held a knife to his face.

The music stopped as The Bard watched in horror. The crowd turned to see what was transpiring, and the room fell into an uneasy hush. Galen swallowed hard as a bead of sweat rolled off his nose and onto the edge of the blade. The Bard squeezed through the onlookers, and stood next to Oranna. "Please, don't do this," he pleaded, a forced smile on his lips. Oranna's expression remained hard as stone. "They're going to give us a room for the night. A good night's rest would be beneficial for our journey tomorrow." Oranna let out a sigh and as quick as the knife had appeared it was stashed away. The room lingered in a tense silence until The Bard laughed awkwardly, "From the top," prompting laughter from the crowd, who resumed their singing.

    Oranna took a long drink and crossed her arms, her expression guarded. Another brave soul took a seat beside her, attempting to break the tension. "Don't mind Galen. He's harmless. A fool, but harmless," he offered. Oranna remained silent, her gaze fixed ahead. Undeterred, the man continued, "I don't mean to pry, but I couldn't help overhearing you will be going on a journey tomorrow?" Oranna glanced at him, but remained tight-lipped. "Well I wager you came into town from the east, heading west. With the Tail looming, are you seeking the mountain pass to the Black Sands of Zola? Curiosity flickered in Oranna's eyes. The man chuckled, nodding towards Ellka. "The little one talks." He shifted his attention back to Oranna. "So, do you have a plan or a map for your journey?"

Oranna inhaled sharply, "I suppose you have one for sale?"

The man let out a laugh. "Gods no," he replied, chuckling. "I can barely write my name. But I have been known to guide people across the Tail to the other side." A grin crept across his face.

Oranna looked at him, her tone resolute. "We will manage on our own, thank you."

Just then, The Bard, out of breath, dropped into a seat. "Oh, good, you've met Avier. He's our host for tonight and will be our guide tomorrow," he said.

Oranna shot a glare at The Bard and muttered through clenched teeth, "We don't need a guide."

The Bard met her gaze with a blank stare. "Don't be ridiculous, Oranna. Avier has been to the pass multiple times. We have nothing to worry about," he insisted.

Ellka chimed in, "And he's giving us supplies."

Reluctantly, Oranna sank in her chair, eyeing Avier. She sighed, "Fine."

"Excellent, looking forward to tomorrow," Avier said, extending his hand.

The Bard enthusiastically embraced him, both men sharing a laugh.

Avier gestured with his hand. "I'll have my brother, Galen, take you over to my place to rest for the night."

Oranna's brow furrowed.

The threesome gathered their belongings, thanked their hosts, and headed to

Avier's house to rest for the night, gearing up for the journey in the morning.

When morning arrived, Oranna had barely slept; an uneasy feeling lingered despite their hosts' absence from the house. The threesome emerged to find Avier, Galen and two ponies loaded with supplies awaiting them. "The day is young," Avier greeted them with a grin. Oranna appeared displeased.

"Ponies!" Ellka squealed with delight. "Can we ride them?" she asked while stroking one.

"They ain't for riding," Galen growled.

Avier grabbed a pack from a pony, lifted Ellka, and placed her on the animal. "There, that should work." he said, winking as a smile beamed from Ellka's face.

"How long till we reach the Mountain pass?" Oranna inquired.

Avier gazed towards the Tail. "Hmm, if the weather holds, two days."

"Then we should get moving." Oranna stated, pushing past them and strided towards the trail.

The Bard stepped beside Avier leaning in close and lifting a bushy eyebrow, whispered, "She didn't sleep well." Avier shrugged, took the reins, and the party began the long hike.

The group soon arrived at the trailhead, finding it heavily overgrown and difficult to advance. Galen pushed himself to the front, carrying a large cleaver. Oranna watched him cautiously as he held it high and chopped away the overgrowth, clearing a path. "Now we go up," he directed, pointing to a rocky path ascending the side of the mountain. Galen led the way, followed by a pony. Behind him trailed The Bard, who spent most of the ascent with his eyes shut, tightly clinging to the wall. Avier came after, guiding Ellka's pony, who was still bobbing and swaying with excitement atop its back. Oranna brought up the rear, she continued to scrutinize the brothers with discerning eyes.

By midday the village was nothing but a small dot over the mountainside. Exhaustion was taking its toll on the group. "Can... we... rest?" panted The Bard between breaths.

"A bit further and we can stop," grunted Galen.

"I want to stop now," whined The Bard as he fell to his knees. At that moment, Avier glanced back, noticing Ellka asleep on the pony. Unaware of The Bard on the ground, he moved forward, inadvertently stepping on him, causing Avier to trip over the side. The Bard screamed as Avier grasped the edge. The pony he was leading reared, and Ellka began sliding off. Oranna swiftly leapt forward, catching Ellka mid-fall. Meanwhile, the pony lost its footing and tumbled over the edge. Its reins, still wrapped around Avier's hand, went taut, and the leather burned as it slipped through his fingers. In a panic, Galen attempted to reach his brother but was blocked by the pony he was leading. "Brother, Hang on!" he yelled. The Bard reached over to assist Avier. Oranna joined him, and together they managed to haul Avier back onto the trail.

Avier glanced down at his bloodied hand. Galen maneuvered around the pony and swiftly came to his brother's side. "Get a clean cloth for his hand," Galen commanded. The Bard went over and cut a few strips of cloth. They gently wrapped Avier's hand, tying it tight to stavethe bleeding. Avier and Galen remained eerily silent, their expressions troubled.

The Bard broke the tension, "What shall we do now?" Galen's eyes burned with rage as he stared at The Bard.

Oranna stepped in between them. "How far till we find level ground to set up camp." Her voice was calm yet firm.

Galen remained silent, "About two miles or so till we reach the first camp." Avier spoke, wincing from the pain. "When we make it there, we can decide what to do." Oranna nodded, casting a glance at the group, but Galen's gaze never left The Bard.

    They trudged on in silence until they reached the small patch of earth. Dark clouds loomed overhead and a chilling wind whipped around them. Galen started setting up his and Avier's tent. The Bard cautiously walked over, "I am truly sorry…" before the words were finished, Galen struck The Bard with a forceful blow that felt like a stone, sending The Bard crashing to the ground, blood gushing from his nose. Galen jumped on top and drew back his fist for another blow. Oranna ran and hooked his arm whirling around him and tossing him into his half constructed tent. Galen regained his footing and drew his knife. "ENOUGH!" Avier screamed, shielding Ellka. "What happened was an accident. It's no one's fault," Avier said, calming his voice. "Brother, finish setting up." Avier approached Oranna, but she spoke first. "I'm sorry for what happened, but your brother needs to control himself before he gets hurt." Avier nodded, "It seems your tent went over with the pony. Once Galen builds this, you three may have it." Galen snorted in response. "We would hate for Ellka to catch anything." Oranna met Avier gaze, "Your kindness is welcomed, but I have my own tent in my bag. It's big enough for Ellka and The Bard. I don't mind this weather." Avier smiled, "As you wish," he bowed, and then helped in setting up the rest of camp.

The next morning, the group worked together to help clean up the campsite and load what they could on the pony. Galen appeared to be in better spirits as they ventured into the mountain canyon. "Today's journey is a long one, filled with twists and turns. Keep up and don't wander, or we may find ourselves lost," Avier advised with a smile. Oranna exchanged a worried look with her companions.

After a few hours of navigating through the rocky maze, The Bard whispered to Oranna, "I don't like this."

Oranna whispered back, "Now you don't? What happened to you trusting them?"

The Bard frowned, "I just don't like following them into this labyrinth."

Oranna smirked, "Perhaps you should lead." The Bard huffed and continued walking.

As the sun rose to its zenith, the group paused for a brief rest. Avier and Galen sat together and left them to themselves. Ellka questioned, "Why don't they sit with us? They aren't speaking to us either. Are they mad?"

Oranna looked at her, feeling a sense of jealousy over her innocence. "They're upset about losing the pony yesterday."

Ellka thought for a moment, "We could buy another one for them." The Bard nearly choked on his food.

"We'll offer to do that when we return," Oranna assured her with a smile.

Suddenly, Avier came over, "We need to keep moving. The weather is shifting, and a fog is setting in. We have a lot more to go through before we can set up camp." They pressed on, and within the hour, a dense fog rolled in, mist began to rain down. For hours, the group struggled to see what was before them. Periodically, Avier would shout to guide them. Soaked and fatigued, they persisted, placing their trust in the brothers.

The air grew thinner, and the cold began to wear on Ellka and The Bard. Oranna drew in a deep breath and caught a whiff of smoke. Alerted, she cautiously drew her knife. They hadn't heard Avier in some time. As they reached a clearing, Avier and Galen had started a fire. Oranna relaxed and sheathed her knife. "Come, warm yourselves. We'll rest here for the night. No need for tents, there's a cave for shelter." Avier pointed to an opening in the rock face. The Bard hurried over and plopped himself down, Avier laughed and Galen prepared a pot of stew.

As nightfall descended on the path, the group gathered round the fire while Galen passed out bowls of warm stew. They ate heartily and sat back with full bellies. Ellka and The Bard soon headed off to sleep in the cave.

Oranna, Avier and Galen stayed by the fire. "Thank you," Oranna said, expressing her gratitude.

"You are most welcome," Avier replied, with his hand over his heart. "If we hadn't volunteered, we'd still be in that hall, listening and retelling the same stories over and over." Galen smiled at his brother. "What made you so eager to travel this way?" Avier inquired.

"Since I was little, I've heard tales of the Black Sands but never have I seen them. I yearn for another adventure before my time ends, and this seemed like a good one." Oranna explained.

Avier nodded, smiling at her response. "I haven't seen them either, but I do know the way. Maybe my journey will continue with you?" Oranna looked up from the fire and within Avier's eyes she saw true sincerity. She nodded and bowed. Avier chuckled softly. "The hour is late, and the journey continues tomorrow. Galen and I will take the first watch. Go now and rest." Oranna stood and dusted herself off. She wrapped a blanket around her and made her way to the cave. As her eyelids grew heavy, her thoughts wandered to the adventures that tomorrow would bring. She drifted to sleep with the fire's glow casting dancing shadows on the cave walls.

When Oranna awoke, it was late morning. She rubbed her eyes and stumbled over The Bard and Ellka, both still fast asleep. Walking into the clearing, she felt confused. "Why didn't you wake me for my watch?" Her eyes adjusted, and she scanned the area. To her surprise, Avier, Galen, and the pony carrying their supplies were gone. The campfire had burnt out, leaving cold coals. Oranna rushed about searching for signs of a struggle or any clue but she found nothing aside from three tracks leading away from camp. She followed the tracks, yet after a few feet the tracks disappeared. With two similar looking ways to go, she returned to camp to find The Bard and Ellka starting to wake up.

"They're gone," Oranna stated firmly.

Ellka yawned and rubbed her eyes "What does that mean?"

"I don't know if they had been planning this all along or if it was a fast decision but they left and took everything." Oranna explained.

The Bard emerged from the cave, "Are you sure? Maybe they just scouted ahead."

Oranna shook her head, "I tracked them out of camp, back along our trail. But they disappeared into the rock. They've left us here to die."

The Bard slumped down in disbelief. "What shall we eat then?" Ellka said, "What shall we drink?" Oranna shrugged, lost in thought.

The Bard glanced at Ellka and then at Oranna, "We have to go back, we can't go any further without guides. You said it yourself, this place is a maze, and we don't know the way." he said, his voice soaked in worry.

Oranna stood, caught between contemplation and shock. Ellka began to cry and The Bard wrapped his arm around her. "Oranna?" The Bard interrupted her thought, "What shall we do?"

She looked at both of them and swallowed, "We move forward." Confusion marked their expressions."I can lead us. I've fought monsters and armies and survived. We can make it through this," she asserted. The Bard began to cry. Oranna knelt beside them, "Trust me. Together, we can find the

Mountain's Edge." She extended her hand, pulling the two of them to their feet.

The threesome gathered whatever supplies they could salvage and set out to find their way. The labyrinthine trails and precipitous cliffs they navigated left them bewildered and disoriented. Each new path offered hope, but the twists and turns only circled them back to the beginning. Despite their attempts to memorize the routes, the rock formations seemed to shift and alter as fog and mist rolled in around them. Hours slipped away, daylight faded, and they found themselves back in the clearing where they began their day. Collapsing to his knees, The Bard wailed, "We shall die here." Ellka copied his actions. Oranna, exhausted, sank down beside the extinguished fire pit. She uncoiled some cord and attempted to strike the rocks together to spark a flame. After several attempts, a feeble glow flickered with little warmth, casting faint shadows on the walls.

During their journey, Ellka had stumbled upon a small nest with a few eggs nestled inside. She threw the nest in the fire as fuel and cooked the eggs for dinner. The threesome ate in somber silence, gathered around the small, flickering fire. The Bard and Ellka huddled together for warmth as the night deepend, while Oranna gazed into the dying embers. As the night wore on and the winds howled, Oranna remained vigilant, keeping watch while the others slept.

When the sun rose the next day, it was a bleak start. Overhead, large gray clouds loomed, and the persistent wind was relentless in its efforts to pierce through their clothes, but the threesome moved on. The Bard, using a candle to mark their path through the rocky labyrinth. At first, this method provided hope, as they moved forward for hours without passing a mark. With hope in their hearts they continued forward. The meager sustenance from the eggs did little to abate their growing exhaustion. Oranna's head throbbed from the pain, she turned to see The Bard staggering and Ellka stumbling to her hands and knees. "Just...a...little further," Oranna struggled to utter the words, her thoughts scattering in her mind. She turned back towards the path before her. Gritting her teeth, she placed one foot in front of the other and stumbled into a clearing. Her vision blurred, as she looked around and her heart sank. All day they had walked in a large circle and now we're back in the same spot. Ellka and The Bard collapsed, and Oranna rolled to her back, crying out a desperate scream. Her voice echoed off the canyon walls and echoed back, taunting her. Overwhelmed and exhausted, her own voice ringing in her ears, she succumbed to unconsciousness.

  As Oranna felt herself slipping away, her senses dulled, and a disorienting tug pulled her as if she was drifting through time and space. Her mind spun, colors of her imagination twisted into a spiral of fear. "Am I dying?" she pondered in her fading consciousness. Unexpectedly, an answer echoed within her mind. "No." Searching around, she found no one near, yet she felt herself from this world to the next. Suddenly, the voice returned, seemingly reading her thoughts. "No, you are not dying. You are in my house, recovering from eating poisoned eggs." The voice, unfamiliar and disembodied, pierced her confusion. With eyes cracked open, she found herself bathed in the soft glow of a fire's light.

In the shadows sat a figure, small and hunched over. Long hair that stood up all over its head, and a thinning beard adorned its face. It moved towards another body lying on the ground, Ellka's figure became distinguishable to Oranna. She reached out and hoarsely spoke, "Don't...hurt...her," before collapsing back into a deep sleep.

When she finally awoke, she looked about her and gently touched her head. A familiar gruff yet sincere voice spoke up, "Awake finally. How do you feel?" She hesitated to answer. Before she could respond, she heard Ellka cry out. Oranna sprang up, her head swimming with dizziness as she lunged for the door. She stumbled but managed to push the door open, revealing Ellka running around a small green space, surrounded by leaves swirling and dancing around her. The owner of the gruff voice came over and helped Oranna to her feet, "There you are now just be careful." In the sunlight, she saw the wrinkled face of an Inalt elf. With pale white, frizzy hair and a long unkempt beard. His clothes were discolored brown and stained with sweat. But his eyes, still an icy blue with a youthful glint, despite his weathered face. He propped her into a chair and gave her a reassuring pat, "I'm Kolvar, but you can call me Kol," he said, sighing cheerfully. Oranna remained confused.

"I live alone up here, far from anyone. I heard a peculiar howl of agony and went searching. Found you and your friends." He gestured toward Ellka playing with the leaves and The Bard watching from a rock. "I noticed that meager fire and the flying snake eggs," he explained. Oranna's eyes widened, and he nodded. "Yep, you all ate flying snake eggs, which everyone should know are poisonous. If I hadn't come along when I did, you all would have probably not made it. But I did and you didn't. Now, let's get your friends in here for some supper." He smiled and called out to her companions.

They all gathered around the table, sitting quietly as Kolvar served up four bowls of soup. Oranna broke the silence, "What is going on." Everyone looked at her curiously. "We were lost in the maze of rocks, we sat upon death's door and you happened along and saved us?" Oranna stood up, drawing her knife. "Who are you, and what are you doing here?"

Kolvar smiled and sat down, "I'm just a hermit that lives in these mountains."

Oranna shook her head, "Lies." Kolvar slurped his soup.

The Bard interjected, "Come now this man saved us. Let's just share some supper and be on our way in the morning. I'm certain he could lead us to the Mountain's Edge."

As the words left his mouth, Kolvar's face turned from joyful to stern. "I will not lead you there cause there ain't nothing to see. Tomorrow I will lead you to the path out of these mountains and be done with you."

Oranna smirked, "I knew you were no good. Why won't you lead us to the Mountain's Edge?"

Kolvar stared at her unblinking, nostrils flaring. Ellka chimed in, "Kol, why won't you help us get to the Black Sands?"

With that, Kolvar's eyes widened and anger grew on his face. He stood abruptly, turning away from the table, "I won't lead you to your death, that is why. Best you eat up and be on your way."

Oranna withdrew her knife and asked again, her voice more curious than interrogative, "Who are you really, Kolvar?"

Kolvar's shoulder shrunk even more, and he drew a deep breath, standing up tall. "My real name is Elnaril, and I was an elven soldier during the Dragon Wars," he revealed. The three of them looked at him in shock. "During that time, I served under Commander Gannondor. He had been tasked with hunting a warband of Orcs and Goblins that had retreated into the mountains. For days, we tracked them through this maze. We had slain most of them, but their leader was fast. We tracked him to the Field of Green Sea, and that is when we saw him." Fear dripped from his voice, "Towering above us was their true leader, Zola the Mountain Giant. But Gannondor showed no fear; we rushed in as he led us with his flaming sword. We slaughtered the Orcs, but Zola managed to make it to the water's edge. I stayed behind with the wounded while Gannondor and a few others pressed on. An hour later, a huge burst of black smoke, fire, and ash shot into the sky. The cloud rained down on us, burning our skin and lungs. The wounded died, and those of us strong enough ran. But it was as if the cloud was alive. It followed us up the mountain and into the maze. I found a small cave and hid. That night, I heard the screams of my friends as it devoured them. By morning, it was gone, retreating back to the beach. I snuck back to the beach in search of any survivors, but there were none. Out of shame and duty, I made my home here to ensure it never leaves." Kolvar dropped to his knees and began to weep.

Ellka walked over and gave Kolvar a hug. Oranna sat back in her chair amazed at what she had just heard. The Bard spoke up, "So how old are you then?" Everyone looked at him, and he shrugged, "I just want to get it correct for my song." Oranna and Ellka exchanged a dismissive glance at the Bard.

Oranna rose and walked to where Kolvar wept. "I know it hasn't been easy for you, and I am sorry we have disturbed your peace, but lead me there, and I can make sure it is gone forever and give you true peace."

Kolvar sat in deep contemplation. "I can't have your blood on my hands."

Oranna lifted his chin, "Then come with me."

Kolvar studied her as though deciphering a code, "Lead me there, and if whatever it is still resides there, we shall destroy it together."

"To what end?" Kolvar replied.

"To bring honor to you and your fallen brothers," Oranna declared. After a while, Kolvar silently rose and left the hut.

Oranna, Ellka and The Bard sat in the hut quietly. Ellka finished her soup and played with the trinkets on a shelf, while Oranna watched out the window. The Bard attempted to weave Kolvar's tale into a song. Suddenly, the door swung open. Ellka's face lit up with delight, and Oranna smiled. There in the doorway was Kolvar, adorned in Ancient Elvish armor. He unsheathed a long sword, its blade sang out as it left its bed. Kolvar gazed upon his old friend and grinned. "Let us restore our honor." The group erupted in cheers, and prepared for the end of their journey.

In the early morning, the group awoke before the sun, and ate a light breakfast, and packed the rest. They gathered their gear and set off down the path from the hut. Kolvar glanced back and gave them a resolute nod. They felt fresh and prepared to finish their journey. By midday, they reached the Mountain's Edge. Before them stretched the horizon and clear blue sky above the Mist Sea. Below them, billowing white clouds rolled over each other as they crashed against the cliff. Beyond was their destiny.

The Bard peered over the edge. "We have to go... down?" Kolvar flashed a mischievous grin. He dropped his bag, retrieved a rope, and effortlessly tied knots into it.

Oranna knelt beside Ellka, "Ellka, When we go down there, I need you to stay hidden. If there is anything dangerous, I need you to run for the cliff ok?" Ellka looked confident and nodded in agreement. Oranna turned to see Kolvar securing the rope to The Bard, "I don't like this." Oranna winked and tied her own rope. Once they were all securely fastened, they began their descent.

The wind whipped Oranna's hair as she rappelled down the cliff. They traversed through the clouds, and below them lay the Field of Green Sea: a deep emerald green expanse of tall grass shimmering and waving as the strong breeze swept across it. The sun hung below the clouds, and the brilliant green mesmerized them.

As they reached the bottom, the sweet smell of the water wafted through the grass, hanging heavy in the air. The ground beneath them was a mixture of sand and dirt, squishing under their feet. Oranna and Kolvar drew their weapons, moving cautiously towards the sound of the crashing water. The Bard and Ellka stayed a few feet behind, remaining on high alert. After a few moments, they entered a clearing, and Kolvar stopped. "What's wrong?" Oranna asked, concerned.

Kolvar pointed to the ground, "This...this is where I abandoned my brothers." At their feet lay the indiscernible remains of the wounded from Kolvar's past.

Oranna placed a hand on his shoulder, "It is not your fault." Kolvar nodded, and they continued on.

The tall grass swished and swayed as they approached the beach. Oranna pushed aside a bunch of grass and then she saw it. The sun hung low, painting the sky with hues of pink, purple and orange. The water appeared a dark gray as the waves crested, churning up the white foam at the shoreline. The sand was jet black against the painted sky. Oranna stood there, mouth agape in awe. The Bard's eyes widened, taking in every detail of the breathtaking sight. Ellka, hands over her mouth, was speechless by the beauty, and Kolvar was visibly moved, a tear glistened down his cheek.

    Oranna knelt down and gathered the sand in her hand, feeling the warmth of the day's sun as the gritty grains passed through her fingers. "It's more beautiful than your songs could ever tell," she exclaimed. The Bard nodded in agreement. The excitement of their journeys end made them giddy. Ellka removed her boots and plunged her feet into the sand and Oranna soon followed. Laughing and cheering, they dashed to the beach and the waters edge, not a care in the world.

Kolvar interjected, "Let's not forget why we're here. Keep your senses about you." Oranna paused from her playful sprint, shaking off the excitement as she readied her blade.

Meanwhile, The Bard strolled carelessly to the water, dismissing their concerns, "You worry too much. Clearly, if something were here, we would see it." Just then, the ground trembled, Ellka turned to see a whirlwind of black sand forming a colossal shape. Two immense sand feet joined by powerful legs, a torso formed atop them, raining sand. Soon, two mighty arms swirled into view with huge fists, followed by a head with two lifeless black eyes and mouth glowing with a fiery intensity. Ellka screamed as the party turned to see their foe.

The Bard rushed over, grabbing Ellka in his arms, and dashed towards the tall grasses to hide. Oranna and Kolvar stood together, both clutching their swords tightly. The Colossus stomped forward, shaking the ground as it moved. It opened its mouth, and a deep, dark voice boomed out, "Who dares wake me from my slumber?"

Kolvar leaned toward Oranna, whispering, "That is Zola."

Oranna stepped forward boldly, "I am Oranna of the North, and I have come to slay you and avenge the Commander Gannondor."

At the mention of the name, The Colossus winced. "Then you have come to die as he did all those years ago," it laughed, causing sand to shake off its body. "How do you expect to defeat me? You don't even have his sword." The Colossus mocked.

Kolvar stepped up, "You mean this?" With a strike on the hilt, the blade glowed red, emanating a heat. "Sunforge lives, and he is hungry for your flesh." Kolvar aimed the blade at The Colossus.

Its eyes widened as it stepped back in fear. As it stepped back both Oranna and Kolvar charged towards The Colossus. Kolvar veered to the right, slashing at its sandy foot. Meanwhile, Oranna threw her knife, and followed it up with a slice to the ankle. Each strike found its mark. Yet, as The Colossus regained its balance, it retaliated by swiping down forcefully, sending sand flying and smashing into both of them. Oranna managed to evade the blow, but Kolvar bore the full force and was flung back, landing prone on the ground. Oranna glanced back, and saw Kolvar rising to his knees. She turned her attention back to The Colossus.

    The Colossus stomped and punched the ground, aiming to crush them. Oranna sliced, but nothing seemed to halt The Colossus's advance. Kolvar rushed in, but The Colossus grabbed Oranna and hurled her at Kolvar. He somersaulted to the side and resumed his assault. The Colossus swung its monstrous leg, slamming into Kolvar, sending him back. He collided with Oranna, and both collapsed on their backs. Oranna rolled Kolvar off her; he laid there motionless. She leaned down, urging, "Kolvar, rise up, I need you!" Kolvar didn't respond. Shaking him gently proved futile as he remained unconscious. Oranna looked back towards The Colossus lumbering towards her.

Once more, she charged at The Colossus, her sword flashing in the fading light. She aimed her strikes at its hands and feet, her barbaric ferocity pouring out like a raging wild bear protecting her cubs. Her anger surged like a tempest. But The Colossus merely looked down and laughed. With both arms, it clapped its hands together, crushing Oranna. Ellka screamed and The Colossus turned its attention towards the grass.

Oranna gathered herself, rising from the ground and staggered forward. Raising her sword, she stood between The Colossus and Ellka, who remained hidden in the grass. As she stood her ground, the hairs on her arms stood up, she felt an otherworldly presence, and then she heard a voice, "Pick up Sunforge."

She turned but found no one there. The voice continued, "Wield Sunforge and strike its heart." Oranna's gaze fell upon Sunforge sticking out of the sand. Stretching her hand out, a vibrant surge of electricity emanated from the hilt. As her fingers grasped the hilt, she felt the smoothness of the pearlescent handle. Retrieving the sword from the sand, the blade sang a song of ancient times. Oranna hit the hilt, and the blade ignited. Determined, she turned and charged The Colossus.

The Colossus swung, and Oranna parried with the blade. To her surprise, the blade sliced through its hand. However, this time it was different, instead of reforming, the sand forming the stump had turned to glass, rendering it unable to regenerate. Astonished by this revelation, Oranna grinned and lunged towards its leg. Soaring through the air, she struck its knee, slicing through. The Colossus hopped back, and seizing the chance, Oranna swiftly slashed the other leg. The Colossus collapsed backward to the ground, causing, it seemed, the earth to shake apart. Oranna leaped onto its chest. As it looked up at her, its remaining hand swung at her. She blocked the attack and sliced in half, from its hand to its elbow. The Colossus shrieked in agony, writhing. Keeping her balance, Oranna jumped, lifting the sword above her head, and brought it crashing down onto The Colossus chest, piercing through the sands and hitting something solid within.

    The blade pierced through the rock shell that was its heart, emitting a sky curdling outcry that echoed across the beach and into the cliffs behind them. Its hollow eyes widened, spewing a white hot light. Oranna pulled the sword from the heart, and fissures cracked like spider webs throughout its body. She leaped from her perch and sprinted towards Kolvar.

    Kolvar, regaining his consciousness, covered himself just before The Colossus exploded. Smoke, ash, and sand soared high into the air and showered down. The force of the blast hurled Oranna through the air, and she tumbled into the sand.

The air cleared, and Kolvar rose to his feet. Scanning the area, The Colossus was gone! Oranna joined Kolvar and handed him Sunforge. He glanced down to find that the blade itself was shattered. "I'm sorry," she offered. Suddenly, a bluish light swirled around them, and as the winds settled, the astral form of Gannondor materialized before them.

"Brother, you have done what I couldn't," it said. Oranna recognized the voice from before, the one guiding her to pick up the sword. "You stayed and brought no shame or dishonor upon yourself." Kolvar dropped to his knees. The spirit turned towards Oranna, "Your strength has ended the curse that haunted these grounds. Thank you." Oranna placed her hand on her heart and bowed. The spirit then addressed Kolvar, "Come with me, brother, your time here is finished." It extended its hand. Kolvar looked up, and placed his hand within the spirit's, and a blue light shimmered, engulfing him. His body transformed into a translucent living spirit, and the two soldiers united. Other spirits of the fallen elves emerged and stood along the entire beach. Kolvar looked at Oranna, and nodded with appreciation. And just as swiftly as they appeared, they vanished.

Oranna stood alone on the beach, gazing down, there in her hand was Sunforge, now repaired and gleaming. Glass remnants of The Colossus sparkled as the final rays of the sun dipped below the horizon. Her disbelief was interrupted by the sound of clapping. Emerging from the grass, The Bard clapped enthusiastically, a look of awe on his face. Ellka ran towards her and sprang into her arms. "That was Amazing!" Oranna chuckled.

The Bard, seizing her face with both hands, kissed her. "I will make so much money from this tale!" Oranna smirked and embraced him warmly.

With the fading sunlight giving way to the darkening night sky, Oranna sighed in relief. They had set up camp and lit a fire on the beach. As she stared up at the stars, a smile graced her lips while Ellka and The Bard attempted to recount the battle.

As she reflected on her journey to the Black Sands, she could never have predicted that this is how it would have ended. A swell of pride and accomplishment left her feeling triumphant and thankful. She had accomplished so much, and now songs of this tale would be sung about her, Oranna of the North, the Giant Slayer.

Acknowledgements

First and foremost, I'd like to thank my wife for her support and patience, as I bounced ideas off her and read to her the many drafts of these stories. I'd also like to thank my daughter for just being a joy, and I hope one day she can experience adventure in this wide world. I'd like to thank God for giving me the talents to write and create. I'd like to thank D&D for inspiring me to write adventures in my own world. I'd also like to thank Matt Brown for his willingness to read and edit my stories, even though it wasn't expected. Lastly, I'd like to thank my partner Isaac for helping develop the World of Talmin that these stories can live in.

If you would like to learn more about our world that we have created, please visit our site: worldoftalmin.fandom.com.

Be on the lookout for many more stories, legends, and encounters. This is only the beginning.

Made in the USA
Coppell, TX
02 February 2024